Leah's heart moved to her throat

as the great whale circled their rubber craft.

Suddenly the whale turned its flukes to the raft and swished it strongly from side to side, with Leah and Cain clinging for their lives. Leah held on to the edges in a death grip, closing her eyes to the terror. Their small raft was tossed like a trembling leaf caught in an autumn windstorm.

A cry of pure terror froze in her lungs. Tense, every cell and muscle alert, Leah began to shake violently. Panic wouldn't allow her to breathe and when she did, the oxygen rasped painfully in her throat. Finally a noise penetrated her dulled senses. A clicking sound, followed by another and another, with the whispered words, "Wow"..."fantastic"..."unbelievable."

Their lives were balancing precariously, at the whim of a fifty-ton whale, and Cain was taking pictures....

Dear Reader,

Although our culture is always changing, the desire to love and be loved is a constant in every woman's heart. Silhouette Romances reflect that desire, sweeping you away with books that will make you laugh and cry, poignant stories that will move you time and time again.

This year we're featuring Romances with a playful twist. Remember those fun-loving heroines who always manage to get themselves into tricky predicaments? You'll enjoy reading about their escapades in Silhouette Romances by Brittany Young, Debbie Macomber, Annette Broadrick and Rita Rainville.

We're also publishing Romances by many of your all-time favorites such as Ginna Gray, Dixie Browning, Laurie Paige and Joan Hohl. Your overwhelming reaction to these authors has served as a touchstone for us, and we're pleased to bring you more books with Silhouette's distinctive medley of charm, wit and—above all—*romance*. I hope you enjoy this book, and the many stories to come.

Sincerely,

Rosalind Noonan
Senior Editor
SILHOUETTE BOOKS

DEBBIE MACOMBER
Yesterday's Hero

Silhouette Romance

Published by Silhouette Books New York

America's Publisher of Contemporary Romance

SILHOUETTE BOOKS
300 East 42nd St., New York, N.Y. 10017

ISBN: 0-373-08426-9

First Silhouette Books printing April 1986

America's Publisher of Contemporary Romance

Printed in the U.S.A.

Books by Debbie Macomber

Silhouette Special Edition

Starlight #128
Borrowed Dreams #241
Reflections Of Yesterday #284

Silhouette Romance

That Wintery Feeling #316
Promise Me Forever #341
Adam's Image #349
The Trouble with Caasi #379
A Friend or Two #392
Christmas Masquerade #405
Shadow Chasing #415
Yesterday's Hero #426

DEBBIE MACOMBER

has quickly become one of Silhouette's most prolific authors. As a wife and mother of four, she not only manages to keep her family happy, but she also keeps her publisher and readers happy with each book she writes.

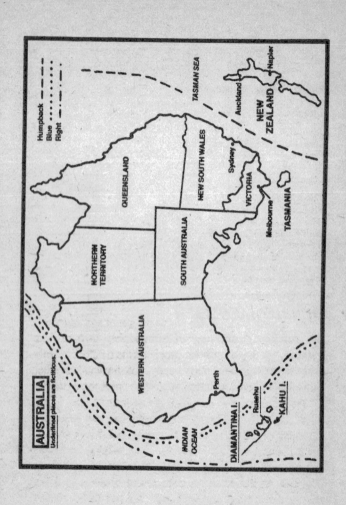

Chapter One

"You must understand that the government of the Diamantina Islands is understandably circumspect. The people are the direct descendants of Puritan missionaries." Dr. David Brewster took a clean handkerchief from his pocket and wiped his perspiring face.

He's flustered, Leah Talmadge mused. Dr. Brewster, California's most renowned marine biologist, man of steel at seventy-five, the solid department head, was obviously nervous. Something had gone wrong. Disconcerted, Leah stiffened in the high-backed leather chair. A cold sweat broke out across her upper lip, and she nervously ran her finger over it. Dear heavens, this expedition was the chance of a lifetime.

"Just what are you saying, Dr. Brewster?" Cain Hawkins interrupted abruptly.

Leah's gaze skidded to the world-famous photographer who would be accompanying her on this whale watch. Cain's work had appeared several times in *National Geographic* and *Life*. The talented photographer had made his name taking spectacular shots of wildlife, landscapes and people; his skill wasn't limited to any one subject. His work hung in some of the best art galleries in the world. The entire department was elated that he'd been assigned to accompany Leah on this expedition to the islands.

His pictures might be fantastic, Leah reflected, but the man was a disappointment. He didn't look anything like what she'd expected. In some ways he resembled a hippie left over from the sixties. His chestnut hair was unfashionably long, and he wore it brushed away from his face. It curled out just below his collar, and an unruly patch defiantly brushed his brow. His face was weathered from exposure to the elements, and he looked closer to forty than the thirty-five she knew him to be. Of course, she'd heard the rumors. Her colleagues had delighted in feeding her tidbits of information about the unorthodox Cain Hawkins. A rebel. A nonconformist. Tough as leather. Hard as nails. Leah had heard it all and secretly hadn't believed a word. His pictures told a different story.

David Brewster paused and cleared his throat. Again he wiped his face with the wrinkled linen cloth. "I was in communication with the governor of the Diamantinas this afternoon."

Apprehensively, Leah scooted to the edge of her seat. "And?" she urged.

"In light of the fact that you two unmarried adults would be spending considerable time in the uninhabited archipelago together, the request has been denied."

Leah felt her heart drop. "Denied," she repeated in shocked disbelief. The opportunity of a lifetime washed away by the moral righteousness of a government official.

"Good grief, man. We live in the twentieth century." Cain Hawkins's dark eyes sparked with disbelief and irritation.

"Indeed," David Brewster agreed, "but no one bothered to inform the islanders of this. These people are deeply religious."

"But, Doctor," Leah said, struggling to disguise her exasperation, "surely you explained that Mr. Hawkins and I are professional people. Our purpose isn't to..." She left the rest unsaid as hot color invaded her pale face. The worst part of being a blonde was the way her complexion signaled her thoughts.

"I fear we must either find a female photographer or make the—"

"Oh no you don't." Cain shot to his feet and glared intimidatingly at Leah, expelling an angry breath. The dark eyes narrowed to points of steel that looked capable of slashing through any barrier, any defense. "You can damn well find a male marine biologist. I'm not giving up this opportunity because of her." An accusing finger was pointed at Leah.

"How...how dare you," Leah stuttered. "I've waited years for this and I won't be denied my chance because—"

"Children, children." Dr. Brewster waved his hand authoritatively.

So angry she could barely speak, Leah defiantly crossed her arms. Whom did Cain Hawkins think he was dealing with, anyway? She hadn't worked this hard and come this far to let a boorish chauvinist walk over her because she was a woman.

"If you two would consider marriage..."

"What?" Leah spat. "Surely you don't mean to each other." Slowly, deliberately, she gave Cain Hawkins a practiced look of distaste.

The corner of his upper lip curled into what she assumed was humorous disdain. He was telling her without words what he thought of that idea.

Leah forced herself to think through this sudden obstacle. Finally she suggested, "Surely, if I were a married woman and Mr. Hawkins a married man—not to each other—then this expedition would be sanctioned by the governor."

David Brewster loosened his tie and ran a finger along the inside of his collar in an agitated movement. "That's a possibility, of course—and, frankly, one I hadn't considered."

"I'm sure that once I talk to Siggy he would be willing to move up our wedding plans."

"Siggy?" Cain repeated, and his voice dripped with sarcasm. "You look like the type of woman who would marry a man named Siggy."

Despite her attempt at disciplined self-control, Leah bit off an angry retort. "Siegfried Harcharik is an honors graduate of MIT and is currently employed as a biochemist for the largest drug company in the

United States." Siggy's credentials, she thought, would quickly put Cain Hawkins in his place. "I consider myself fortunate to be his fiancée."

Cain's low snicker filled the room. "Honey, if I were you, I'd consider myself lucky to be any man's future wife."

The words came at Leah like the cutting edge of a sword, and with as much power to inflict pain. She hated herself for wincing. No one needed to remind her that though she was blond she wasn't beautiful. Too tall. Too thin. Too...no need fencing around the word...ugly. From the time she was in junior high she'd known her uneven features weren't likely to attract a male. All brains, no beauty, was what the boys in high school used to say.

Standing, Leah clenched her hands together in a show of determination. "I can see that Mr. Hawkins and I are only capable of hurling insults at each other. I suggest we schedule a meeting for a later date. Tomorrow, perhaps, when we've both had the opportunity to cool our tempers."

"I couldn't agree more." David Brewster's pained, wrinkled face relaxed. "Shall we say Thursday at the same time?"

"Fine." The clipped response was followed by the scraping of a chair as Cain left the room.

Leah avoided looking in his direction and lingered in the office an extra moment.

"My dear," Dr. Brewster said, and cupped Leah's elbow. "I know this announcement has come as a surprise to us all. But I personally chose you for this whale expedition, and I won't easily be dissuaded. So rest assured, things will work out."

Leah's returning smile was feeble at best. "Thank you, Doctor." She didn't know that she should be all that reassured. Dr. Brewster had also handpicked Cain Hawkins.

"I'll talk to Siggy tonight."

"You do that," he returned, patting her back. "I'm confident we'll find a way around this."

Leah was skeptical, but she gave him a polite nod on her way out the door.

The long drive down the San Diego Freeway was accomplished by rote. Traffic, smog, faceless people were all part of life in southern California. Leah learned early that she must either accept it, or be defeated by the congestion that met her morning and night. But this afternoon, California had never seemed farther from the rolling hills of wheat in her home state of South Dakota. It had been a long time since she'd visited her family. When she returned from the Indian Ocean she'd make a point of doing that.

The first thing Leah did when she entered her condominium was pull Cain Hawkins's book of photographs from the shelf beside the fireplace. With a sense of incredulity, she ran her fingertips over the bottom of each page. The photos were beautiful. Each one looked as if the man who took it was revealing his soul.

But Cain Hawkins wasn't anything like these pictures. The ruthless quality in him had astonished her. In her mind, she had formed an image of what he would be like. Not so much his looks, but his personality. Any man who could reveal so much with his camera must be capable of deep insight. Today she had learned that he was ordinary. Hurtful. Arrogant. And, indeed, insightful. Within fifteen minutes of their meeting, he had found her weakest point and attacked.

Angry with herself for letting his cutting words disturb her so much, Leah picked up the telephone and dialed Siggy's work number.

The line rang only once. "Harcharik here."

"Siggy, it's Leah." A short silence followed her announcement.

"Hello, darling."

Leah knew Siggy didn't like it when she phoned him at the office, but she couldn't help it. This was important. "Can you stop by for a few minutes after work?"

Again he hesitated. Siggy had never been one to move quickly on anything. The trait was part of the scientist in him. "Yes, I suppose I could."

In her mind Leah could see him pushing up the bifocals from the bridge of his nose, and she smiled softly, appreciating him.

"Good, I'll see you then. Goodbye, darling." The word stuck in her throat. So far in their relationship, they'd never done anything more intimate than call each other darling, and that had troubled her from the beginning. But the time was fast approaching when she'd be far more intimate with him. She liked Siggy. No, she corrected herself mentally, she loved Siggy. She wanted to be his wife. They shared so many of the same interests. They were perfect for each other. Everyone said so. And Leah was the first woman Siggy had introduced to his family that his mother approved of. That said a lot.

After tucking Cain's book back onto the shelf, Leah delivered her briefcase to her small office in the back of the condominium. For the hundredth time in as many days, she read over the Australian government's report of the sighting of an ancient whale. The report had been received with a high amount of skepticism since ancient whales were assumed to be extinct.

But when the corpse of an ancient whale had been found washed up on one of the Diamantina Islands, the world had taken serious note. Scientists from all over the globe had converged on the tiny cluster of islands a thousand miles southwest by south of Australia and found nothing. Now, a year later, Leah was going during migration time, when she could study the herds and keep meticulous records. This was more than a golden opportunity; it was one that wasn't likely to be repeated.

By the time Siggy arrived Leah had released her tightly coiled hair so that it cascaded down the middle of her back. Siggy had always loved her hair down. She prayed now that it would be all the inducement she needed for him to agree to her plans.

"Hello, darling." He brushed his lips across her cheek.

"Come in." Nervously, Leah gestured toward the fashionably furnished living room. "Would you like something to drink? Coffee's on."

"That'll be fine."

With Siggy, Leah was forced to wear flat-heeled shoes. He exactly equaled her five-foot-eight stature and disapproved when she wore anything that made her taller. And although he claimed to like her hair worn down, Leah sometimes wondered if it wasn't that, with the blond length piled on her head, it gave an illusion of height. Not that any of this mattered; she was happy to do anything to please Siggy.

"I had a meeting with Dr. Brewster and Cain Hawkins today," she said, forcing a casual note into her voice as she delivered his coffee.

"Yes, I remember your saying something about that. How did it go?"

Sitting across from him on the white leather couch, Leah expelled a shaky breath. "Not so well."

"Why not? Isn't this Hawkins fellow what you expected?"

"Not at all." She pushed the hair away from her face. "Siggy, has it ever bothered you...I mean, have you ever been concerned about the fact that I'll be spending several weeks alone with an unmarried man?"

Straightening the corner of his bow tie, Siggy stiffened slightly. "Of course not. You're going to be my wife, Leah. I trust you implicitly."

Leah's heart softened, and she gave him a loving look. "Oh, Siggy, you're so good for me."

His returning smile was brief. "You are for me too, darling." Fidgeting, he glanced at his wristwatch, then cleared his throat. "Mother's holding dinner."

"Oh...well, the reason I asked you over tonight was..." she began, and her hands were so tightly clenched she felt the blood supply must be cut off. Suddenly Leah felt unsure that she was doing the right thing. Marriage, after all, was forever. "I've been thinking that I'd like us to be married before I leave for the Diamantina Islands." Leah watched him closely, but no emotion showed in his blue eyes.

"Leah, I'm afraid that's quite impossible. Mother doesn't know yet that I've asked you to be my wife."

"Then don't you think it's time Mother did?" she said crossly. "You told me yourself that your mother approved of me. I can't see the necessity of putting my life on hold because you're afraid of your mother."

His coffee cup made a clanking sound as he set it roughly on the coffee table. As far as Leah could remember, this was the most emotion she had ever seen from Siggy. "I find that comment unforgivable."

The flaxen length of Leah's hair fell forward as she bowed her head. "Maybe you should leave then. I wouldn't want you to be late for dinner with Mother."

Standing, Siggy straightened his pants legs. "I don't know what's come over you, Leah. You're hardly the girl I fell in love with anymore."

"Woman," she corrected brittlely. "I'm not a little girl who can live on promises. I'm a woman."

Her back was ramrod straight as Siggy walked across the carpet and paused at the door. "I'll phone you tomorrow. You'll have come to your senses by then."

Refusing to answer, Leah pinched her mouth tightly closed until her teeth hurt. Her lashes fluttered closed when the front door clicked, telling her that Siggy had left. Frustration came in waves, lapping at her from all

sides, until she wanted to lash out at anyone or anything. Naturally, she didn't.

An hour later, disheartened and miserable, Leah
tossed a TV dinner into the oven and set the timer. The
local evening news was blaring from the TV when the
doorbell chimed. Leah's heartbeat quickened. Siggy
had reconsidered.

She fairly flew to the door, but her welcoming smile
died an instant death when she saw it was Cain Hawkins and not Siggy.

"Can I come in?" he asked brusquely, and pa-
raded past her, not waiting for a response.

"Feel free," she returned mockingly. "Make yourself at home while you're at it." She stepped aside and
closed the door with her back, suddenly needing its
support. "What can I do for you?"

"You and I have to reach an understanding."

"I'm going, Mr. Hawkins. There is nothing on
God's green earth that's going to keep me from the
Diamantinas."

Cain jerked a hand from his pants pocket and ran
it through the dark hair along the side of his head.
"Me either, lady."

Lady! Well, at least that was an improvement over
Siggy, who apparently viewed her as a disobedient
child.

"Did you talk to this Sidney fellow?" he demanded, pacing in front of the sofa.

"Siggy," Leah corrected calmly, still standing at the
front door.

"Whoever." Impatiently, his hand sliced the air.

"Yes, as a matter of fact I did discuss the situation with Siggy." Primly, Leah folded her hands. She wasn't about to announce to this arrogant male that Siggy hadn't asked his mother's permission yet.

His hand returned to the corduroy pocket. "I don't suppose you've got a beer?"

"You're right. I don't."

He gave a look that said he'd guessed as much. "Well, what did ol' Sidney say?"

Leah lowered her gaze. "He's...he's thinking about it. And it's Siggy," she returned with marked patience.

"Whoever," they said together in perfect unison.

For the first time, Leah saw Cain smile. Despite everything she felt about this man, she had to admit she liked his smile. His whole rugged face was affected by the movement of his mouth. His eyes grew a richer shade of brown until they looked almost black, and she saw a glimpse of the man she'd always thought him to be.

"Did I hear something ding?" Cain turned his ear toward the kitchen.

Leah nodded. "Yes. Please excuse me a minute."

He followed her into the compact kitchen and idly leaned against the counter as she opened the oven door and took out the foil-covered meal.

"You don't honestly eat that garbage, do you?" he asked, his voice rising with astonishment. "Good grief, no wonder you're so thin. Come on, I'll take you to dinner and feed you properly. You need some meat on those bones."

Leah bristled. "How could I possibly turn down such a flowery invitation?" she asked with more than a trace of sarcasm.

"Right." A reckless grin slashed his mouth. "How could you?"

The next thing Leah knew, she was being ushered out the front door and into the lot where a red Porsche speedster was parked.

Stopping, Leah ran her hand along the polished surface of the car and shook her head knowingly. "Honestly, Hawkins, you're so predictable."

He mumbled something under his breath and left her to open her own door and climb inside.

Leah had barely snapped the seat belt into place when Cain revved the engine and shoved the gear into place. They left the parking lot with a spray of gravel kicking up in their wake. The tires screeched as they came to the first red light.

"Do you have to... is it necessary to drive quite so fast?" Leah asked, holding on to the seat with both hands.

"Just wait. This baby does one eighty-five."

"Not with me, it doesn't." Leah reached for the door handle to climb out, but the light changed and Cain shot across the intersection like a bullet out of a gun. Leah's head was jerked back with such force that it bounced against the headrest.

"Isn't this great?"

"No." Leah screamed, instinctively reaching for the dashboard. Her heart was pounding so fiercely she didn't know which was louder, her pulse or the roar of the engine.

Suddenly, Cain slowed down to a crawl and laughed. That mocking, taunting laugh Leah hated. She was so angry, she couldn't breathe.

"Now." He pulled over to the curb and parked. "Isn't that what you expected? You took one look at my car and immediately assumed that I was a crazy man at the wheel."

Unable to answer, Leah placed her hand over her heart and shook her head.

Cain's fingers tightened around the steering wheel. "We'll get along a lot easier if you learn something right now, lady. I'm never predictable. I do what I want, where I want and when I want. Got it?"

The grip on her anger was so fragile that Leah's voice shook dangerously. "Don't ever do that to me again. And...and you get one thing straight. I have a name, and it isn't lady or honey or princess. It's Leah." Her shoulders were heaving, her breasts rising with every panting breath.

Their eyes locked, hers filled with determination and pride, his with an unreadable quality she couldn't quite define. She hoped it was grudging respect. When his hands loosened their grip on the steering wheel, she relaxed.

"Hello, Leah, my name is Cain Hawkins." He extended his hand to her, and with a trembling smile she placed her much smaller one in his.

"Hello, Cain."

A smile briefly touched his commanding features before he checked the side mirror and pulled back onto the street. "I hope you're hungry," he said with a laugh.

"I don't know." Leah's returning laugh was shaky. "I think you might have to go back the way we came. My stomach is about a mile behind us."

He didn't laugh; his concentration was fixed on the road. Trying not to be obvious, Leah studied him from beneath long lashes. He was a complicated man, and she doubted that anyone could truly understand him. A genius. Few would deny that. For the first time she noticed a small dimple in his cheek. It wasn't apparent except when his face was relaxed, Leah concluded. His hair was unkempt and his beard showed a five o'clock shadow. She wondered if he often forgot to shave, then smiled because she knew intuitively that he did.

They arrived at an Italian restaurant that emitted the aroma of pungent spices and tomatoes. It seemed like weeks since Leah had eaten a decent meal.

Cain was recognized immediately, and there were shouts from the kitchen as a short, stout man came through the swinging doors, wiping his hands on a white apron. A flurry of Italian flew over Leah's head.

The man from the kitchen, whom Cain called Vinnie, directed his attention to Leah and nodded approvingly. He shook his head dramatically, his white teeth gleaming.

Never had Leah felt more as if she was standing on an auction block. Nervously she tucked a strand of hair around her ear and shifted her weight from one foot to the other.

A woman with a lovely olive complexion appeared, her dark hair filled with strands of silver. She too joined in the conversation, then slapped her hands with apparent delight.

Leah recognized only a few words of Italian, but *bambino* was one of them. Leah surmised that the restaurant couple were expecting their first grandchild and offered them a smile of congratulations.

Smiling happily, the woman took Leah by the shoulders and nodded her head several times. Again a flurry of Italian was followed by laughter.

When Cain put his arm around her shoulder, bringing her close to his side, Leah was all the more confused.

The couple led Cain and Leah into a secluded corner of the restaurant and smiled broadly as they held out the chairs. Almost immediately, a flurry of activity commenced. A large loaf of freshly baked bread and a thick slab of cheese were delivered to the table.

"You speak Italian," Leah said to break the silence between them. It wasn't one of her more brilliant deductions.

"I picked it up as a kid in Europe," Cain explained, pulling apart a hunk of bread and cutting off a slice of cheese.

Leah followed his example, taking a smaller piece of both the bread and the cheese. "You were born in Europe?" She wouldn't have guessed it.

"No, I was an Army brat. My dad was stationed all over the world. My mother and I were with him much of the time."

"How interesting." Leah realized her comment sounded trite, and she regretted having said anything.

"Actually, I was born in California, but soon afterward we were stationed in Formosa." He paused and took a sip of wine. "That's Taiwan now."

She knew that much from Trivial Pursuit.

"What about you?"

Her fingers worked the stem of the wineglass. "I'm originally from South Dakota. My father's a farmer. Wheat, barley, soybeans, that kind of thing." She didn't mention how much she loved Cain's photos of America's farmlands and how she'd given that book to her father for Christmas last year.

If Cain was surprised by her homey, Midwest background, he didn't show it. But Leah was quickly learning that Cain didn't divulge anything unless it suited him. Something told her that he usually didn't talk about himself. Even in his books there was little information given about him. Most of what she knew she'd heard through gossip.

The bread and cheese disappeared, to be replaced with a relish plate filled with crisp, fresh vegetables and dark olives. Their wineglasses were replenished.

"You must come here often." Leah felt as if she had to carry the conversation. The looks Cain was giving her were unsettling. His thick brows were drawn together as if he were seeking something beyond her obvious lack of beauty. Either that, or something was troubling him. Lowering her eyes, she cursed their color for the thousandth time. They weren't quite green, nor dark enough to be brown, but some murky shade between.

She reached for a celery stick, then laid it against the side of her plate. Opening her mouth would only have drawn attention to how full her lips were.

"Your eyes are the most unusual color," Cain commented thoughtfully.

Leah's hand gripped the linen napkin in her lap. "Yes, I know." It looked for a minute as if Cain would say something else, but the waiter interrupted to deliver a small salad covered with a creamy herb dressing.

"You obviously know these people," Leah tried again.

"We go way back."

That absent, thoughtful look was back, and if Leah didn't know better she'd have said he was nervous about something. "I thought you must. They were saying something about a baby. Are they expecting a grandchild?"

Cain regarded her blankly. "No."

Leah's fork played with a lettuce leaf. "Oh, I thought I heard her say *bambino*, but then I'm not exactly fluent in Italian."

"You did," he said, but he didn't elaborate.

The salad was taken away and quickly followed by a plateful of spaghetti with a thick, rich meat sauce.

"I don't know if I can eat all this," Leah said with a wistful sigh.

A half smile deepened the grooves on one side of his face. "Be sure and save room for the main course."

"The main course," Leah repeated, her round eyes giving him a shocked look.

"I guess I should have warned you." His smile was replaced with a frown of concentration as he wove the long strands of spaghetti around his fork, using his spoon as a guide.

Leah watched him for a minute and shook her head, unwilling even to attempt his method. Setting her fork aside, she studied Cain. There was something bothering him. She could sense it in the way his brow knitted as he manipulated the spaghetti.

Cain looked up and their eyes clashed. "What's wrong?" she asked softly.

Cain heaved a sigh and set his fork aside. "Damn, I'm no good at this."

Leah blinked uncertainly. Good at what? she wondered.

"I thought if I created a romantic mood it would help. But, hell, I don't go in for this romance garbage."

Leah was stunned into speechlessness. She'd never thought of herself as stupid, but at the moment she felt incredibly so. Cain looked as if he wanted to punch a hole in the wall, and she hadn't an inkling why.

"You know what's going to happen Thursday, don't you?"

She shook her head, more confused than ever.

"Brewster's going to come up with a compromise team."

Forcefully, Leah shook her head. "He wouldn't do that." He couldn't. David Brewster knew how much this trip meant to her.

"Of course he would. It's the only answer. If he doesn't he takes the risk of offending us both. And whether he feels like admitting it or not, we're both valuable to the university.''

It didn't take much thought for Leah to recognize that what Cain was saying was true.

"And, damn it—" he tossed his napkin onto the table "—you may have this Sidney fellow to solve your problems, but there isn't anyone I can marry at the drop of a hat.''

Leah couldn't believe that. "What . . . what are you suggesting?''

"There's only one thing to do." Cain looked thoroughly miserable. He reached for his wine and took a gulp. "Leah . . . ?" He hesitated.

"Yes.''

"Damn it anyway. Will you marry me?''

Chapter Two

"Marry...you," Leah repeated, dumbfounded.

"It isn't like this is any love match," Cain inserted, clearly angry. "We're adults. How old are you, anyway?"

"Twenty-eight." That, at least, was easily enough answered.

Cain looked surprised. "You look younger. I checked with a judge friend of mine this afternoon and found out all we need is blood tests. We can have those done tonight, get the license and be married before your first class in the morning."

"I...I suppose we could." A caldron of doubts bubbled in her mind, but Leah could marshal no argument. Cain was right. They were adults, they were professional people and they both desperately wanted to be a part of this expedition. The choice was clear.

"Does that mean yes?" Cain demanded.

Leah chose to ignore the warning lights blinking in her brain. "Yes," she murmured.

"Thank God," Cain said with an exaggerated sigh. He called out something in Italian, and the entire kitchen staff appeared. Someone brought out an accordion, and the man Cain had called Vinnie pumped Cain's hand and kissed him on both cheeks.

Music filled the restaurant. Violins, accordions, guitars. Champagne flowed freely, and Leah quickly lost count of the number of people who congratulated her with kisses on both cheeks. It seemed she waltzed with more men in that one night than she had in her whole life.

The next thing she remembered was Cain delivering her to her apartment and asking her if she was going to be sick. The whole world was singing and dancing, spinning and weaving, and it was all she could do to wave him aside. Leah didn't know if she was going to be sick or not. But if she was, she didn't want Cain around.

The next morning Leah awoke in the clothes she'd worn to dinner the night before. She was suffering from the worst headache of her life. The base of her skull was throbbing as if an avenging demon were hammering on it.

Leah staggered into the bathroom and brushed her teeth but the sound of running water only intensified the ache in her head, and she turned off the faucet. Pressing a hand against her forehead, she took in deep breaths and winced when the doorbell chimed. With her hand still to her head, she moved to the living room and, as quietly as possible, undid the dead bolt lock and opened the front door.

"Morning," Cain greeted her stiffly. "How do you feel?"

"About the same as I look," she whispered.

Idly he stuck his hands in his pockets and cocked his head to one side. "That bad, huh?"

Leah gave him a frosty glare. "I just woke up. I'd like to shower and change first."

"Sure. Do you mind if I make myself a cup of coffee?"

In her worst nightmares she had never dreamed that her wedding day would be anything like this. Cain wasn't even wearing a suit. He was dressed casually in dark cords and a sport shirt. She watched as he removed his leather coat and draped it over the kitchen chair, then paused to look at her expectantly. "The coffee?"

"Go ahead. The can is in the cupboard above the stove."

She left him to his own devices while she surveyed the contents of her closet. She didn't have a thing to wear. And the urge to use that as an excuse to back out of the wedding was almost overwhelming. Finally she chose an olive-green dress. The color matched her mood.

The shower took some of the ache from her bones, but the whine of the hair dryer nearly drove her insane. Before twisting the blond strands into her usual chignon, Leah stepped into the kitchen. Cain was at the table reading the morning newspaper.

"Would you prefer my hair up or down?" she asked as she poured herself a cup of coffee.

Cain glanced up and blinked. "Would I what?"

"My hair," she returned with marked patience. "Should I wear it up or down? Siggy prefers it down."

Cain's blank stare continued. "Good grief, why should I care? You could be bald and it wouldn't make any difference."

Leah successfully resisted the urge to shout at him that this whole thing was ludicrous and she wouldn't have anything to do with it. "I'll leave my hair down then."

"Fine." Already his attention had reverted to the newspaper.

Leah had hardly taken more than a few sips of her coffee when Cain straightened and checked his watch. "The courthouse is open. Let's get this over with."

"Before we do anything with legal ramifications, I think we should make certain aspects of this relationship clear," Leah asserted.

"Of course." Cain gave her a strange look. "I've already thought of that." He lifted his coat from the chair and took out a folded piece of paper. "Read this over and see if I've left out anything."

Scanning the list, Leah was impressed with his thoroughness. Everything she'd thought to mention was there. She didn't want him to have any legal claim to her assets, and she wanted to keep her surname. "I'd like the divorce proceedings to start the first week after our return instead of a month later."

Cain hesitated. "Fine. Write that in if you want, but I can't have my time tied up in court. I'll be working day and night developing the film."

"I'm sure it will be a relatively painless process." Leah spoke with more confidence than she was feeling. "If it would make things simpler, we could make a quick trip into Nevada."

Again Cain glanced at his watch. "Let's decide that later."

"Fine," was Leah's clipped response. He didn't care how she styled her hair, and she didn't care how they went about the divorce as long as there was one.

"You'll notice that I've left a space for each of us to sign. You can keep a copy and I'll take the other."

"Good." Leah penned her name in flowing, even strokes and handed the ballpoint to Cain, who scribbled his signature below hers.

"You ready now?" he asked.

Leah answered him by reaching for the short olive jacket that matched her dress.

Obtaining the license was a simple matter of handing the clerk the results from the blood tests, penning their signatures and paying the fee. Leah watched the money change hands and felt they were selling themselves cheap.

Recognizing how strange it would sound, Leah resisted questioning the clerk about where they could file for the divorce. That would be easy enough to find out when they returned from the Diamantinas.

Judge Preston's quarters were in the same building, only a matter of a short ride in the elevator.

Leah paused outside the door, staring at the evenly printed letters on the glass door. Nervously, her fingers toyed with the strap of her purse as she bit into her quivering bottom lip.

Cain opened the door and pressed a hand in the small of her back, urging her forward. "Come on," he said impatiently, "we're running on a tight schedule."

Squaring her shoulders, Leah stepped into the office. Her throat was desert dry with apprehension.

"Judge Preston is expecting us," Cain announced to the receptionist.

The attractive young woman flashed them an easy smile. "You must be the young couple the judge mentioned this morning. He asked me to be your witness. That is, if you don't mind?" She directed her questions to Leah.

Both the receptionist and Cain seemed to be waiting for Leah to respond. "That's very kind...thank you."

They were ushered into the judge's quarters, and the gray-haired, fatherly-looking man stood immediately. "Welcome, my boy. It's good to see you." Enthusiastically, he shook Cain's hand and turned to Leah. "You've chosen well, Cain. Your father would be proud." He centered his attention on Leah and smiled at her with blue eyes that had faded with age but retained their sparkle. Taking her cold, clammy hand in his, he said, "There's no need to be nervous. Cain Hawkins took his time in choosing a bride. He'll make you a good husband."

Obviously Cain hadn't explained the situation to anyone, and Leah was supposed to fall in with this happy-bride act.

Leah saw Cain glance at his watch, and she seethed silently. If he announced once more that they were on a tight schedule, she swore, she was going to turn around and walk out that door.

The judge leaned forward and flipped a switch on the intercom. "We're ready now, Joyce. Would you ask Mr. Graham to step into my office?"

At Cain's look of surprise, the judge explained. "Your other witness."

Cain looked uncomfortable as he took the license from his coat pocket and gave it to his friend.

As soon as everyone was in their place, the judge reached for his little black book and flipped through the pages.

"We are gathered here today..."

The words droned in Leah's ear as she struggled to pay attention. This wasn't right. Marriage was forever, a commitment meant to last a lifetime. Her parents had recently celebrated their thirtieth wedding anniversary. Divorce was such an ugly word. No one in her family had ever been divorced. Panic grew within Leah until she wanted to turn and bolt from the room and Cain Hawkins's craziness. Nothing was worth compromising everything that she believed was right.

"Do you take this man to be your lawfully wedded husband, in sickness and in health...?"

"I don't know," Leah cried, desperately close to tears.

Four stunned faces turned to her. Cain looked as if he wanted to wring her neck, and she couldn't blame him. Leah swallowed and fought back the rising hysteria. "It just doesn't seem right to talk about divorce on the way to the wedding. I . . . I was raised to believe in the sanctity of marriage."

"Leah," Cain's low voice threatened, "we agreed."

"I know." Her newly discovered resolve was faltering.

"Think of the whales," he whispered enticingly.

Dear Lord, she loved those marvelous creatures. Her hazel eyes pleaded with Cain to understand.

"Miss Talmadge," the judge spoke gently. "If you have any questions about this ceremony . . ."

Cain's eyes sharpened with determination. "There's no problem. Carry on."

"Miss Talmadge?"

Leah could feel Cain stiffen at her side. His hand at the back of her waist pressed into her painfully. She couldn't believe he was hurting her consciously.

"Leah," Cain urged.

"I do," she screamed. "All right, all right, I'll go through with it."

A minute later a recognizably flustered judge asked for the ring. Cain and Leah looked at each other with growing frustration. They'd completely forgotten the wedding bands.

In an apparent move to stall for time while he thought of something, Cain pretended to search through his pockets.

"I think we may have left those at Leah's apartment," Cain murmured, and gave Leah a panicked look.

"You can borrow mine," the receptionist offered generously, slipping the small diamond ring from her finger.

"No...I wouldn't want to do that." Marrying under these circumstances was difficult enough; Leah refused to borrow a ring. "Molly Brown wore a cigar band," she offered, hoping to lighten the mood.

"Who?" The same four faces glared at her.

She swallowed uncomfortably. "*The Unsinkable Molly Brown*...it was a movie with Debbie Reynolds several years ago."

"Will this do?" The young attorney who was standing next to Cain withdrew a pull tab from a soda can out of his pocket. "As I understand the law, a ring isn't actually required. This will do until you replace it later."

"Good idea." Cain brightened. "Thanks."

Fifteen minutes later, Cain and Leah were on the freeway, heading toward Leah's apartment.

"Well, that wasn't so bad, was it?" Cain broke into the oppressive silence that filled the car.

"Not bad?" Leah returned, shocked. "It had to be the most horrible experience of my life."

"You're letting your emotions get in the way. The little girl in you is waiting for orange blossoms and the flowing white gown and veil. You can have that the next time."

Leah wanted to hate him for being so analytical. None of this had troubled Cain.

"I...I don't care what you say, I don't feel right about this."

"Honestly, Leah, it isn't like we did anything wrong."

"Then why am I filled with regrets? Why is there a lump in my throat and I feel I could cry?"

"Oh, good grief, here it comes."

Leah ignored him as best she could. If she couldn't disregard Cain's sarcasm, she'd end up looking for some painful way to lash out at him. "We were wrong to have married like this. And whether you admit it or not, we've lost something we'll never be able to recapture."

Cain stopped at the light at the bottom of the exit ramp and thumped his fingers against the steering wheel. "You've been a good sport until now. Don't go melodramatic on me."

Staring straight ahead, Leah murmured caustically, "Right."

Cain came to a halt beside her car in the parking lot. She slipped the ridiculous soda can ring from her finger and left it on the console.

"I'll stop by tonight," Cain said as he leaned across the car seat when she climbed out. "We've got lots to discuss."

Leah couldn't think of a thing she had to say to him.

"About the trip," he said, apparently having read her thoughts. "I'll see you about seven. Okay?"

She never wanted to see Cain Hawkins again. "All right," she found herself agreeing.

Leah's classes that day were a disaster. It would have been better to have phoned in sick, for all the good she did. Her mind refused to function properly, and she made several embarrassing mistakes. All she seemed able to think about was that this morning she had married a man she didn't know, who was probably the coldest, least demonstrative, most analytical being on earth. Cain Hawkins's pictures may have been wonderful, but they were nothing like the man.

As promised, Cain was at her apartment at seven, bringing a six-pack of beer with him. He delivered it promptly to the refrigerator.

"Feel any better?" he asked on his way out of the kitchen.

"No," she answered stiffly. She was about to tell him what he could do with his beer, when he spoke.

"This should improve your mood." He took a plain gold wedding band from his pocket. When she ignored it, he reached for her hand and pressed it into her palm. "It was my mother's."

The ring warmed her hand, and Leah realized he must have been holding it for quite some time before giving it to her. Leah stared at it, unable to believe Cain would do something like this. "I . . . I appreciate the thought, but I don't want your mother's ring."

"What am I going to do with it, anyway?"

Leah gave him a look of disbelief. "Someday there'll be a woman you love that you'll want to give this ring to." Someone beautiful, no doubt, she added silently.

Cain removed his jacket and tossed it over the leather love seat. "If I can go thirty-five years avoiding the marriage trap, then . . ."

Leah started to giggle. She couldn't help it. Laughter consumed her, and she covered her mouth. Giant tears welled in her eyes and rolled down her pale cheeks.

"What's so all-fired funny?"

"You . . . us," she managed between peals of laughter. "Avoiding the marriage trap, indeed. You *are* married. *We're* married."

His mouth was pinched as he went back into the kitchen and returned with a can of beer. "Wear the ring. You'll need to have one or there'll be questions."

"But not your mother's ring." Leah watched him with mounting incredulity. Maybe he didn't care. Apparently there was little in life that did concern him.

"Yes," he insisted tightly. "My mother's ring. What do I want with it?"

His face tightened with anger. Or perhaps it was pain; Leah couldn't tell.

"It's obvious this sort of thing means something to you," he continued. "So keep it."

"Don't you care about anything?" Leah asked, perplexed by this complicated man. True, the ring wasn't worth much, but it must have had some sentimental value if he'd kept it all these years.

"I care about a lot of things," he countered swiftly. "Good beer." He saluted her mockingly by raising the aluminum can. "And gourmet food, which reminds me, have you eaten yet?"

"Stop it," she shouted unreasonably. For the first time since they'd met, Leah felt she was close to understanding this man. So this was how he'd remained single all these years. He allowed people to get only so close before shutting them out. Cain Hawkins was running from life, from commitment, from everything that his photographs revealed. Only when he was behind a camera was he comfortable.

"I take it you ate," he prompted.

She hadn't been able to down anything all day. "No."

"Good. Why don't you throw two of those aluminum meals in the oven? I could eat a cow."

Ignoring him, Leah fingered the plain gold band. Cain hadn't fooled her. The ring meant a great deal to him, and he was giving it to her to prove to himself in some perverse way that it meant nothing.

"I can't accept this," she said, holding out the ring.

Cain looked stunned. "Why not? It isn't like it was all that important to my mother." He laughed mirthlessly. "She left it on the kitchen counter when she ran off."

Just by the way his voice dipped to a low, husky tone, Leah realized how painful that episode must have been for Cain. "But you kept it?" she prompted softly.

"No." He took a long drink from his beer. "My father did. I found it recently when I was going through Dad's things." A glazed look flitted across his face as he explained softly, "He died six months ago."

"I'm sorry."

"Why? Was it your fault?" The sarcasm laced through his words said she was getting too close and it was time to push her away. He took another swig of his beer and took a small pad from his coat pocket.

Leah moved into the kitchen, turned on the oven and popped two "aluminum meals" inside. The ring sat on the white countertop and magnetically drew her attention. No matter where she was in the kitchen, her gaze was attracted to it. Finally, she picked it up and slipped it on her finger. The fit was perfect.

In a way she couldn't explain, Leah *felt* married. And although they'd only met a day ago, there was a bond between them. A spiritual bond. Cain didn't go around telling people about his mother, she was convinced of that. Nor would he mention to a mere acquaintance that his father had recently passed away.

When they'd agreed to get married, neither of them had expected it to have any effect on their lives. Not really. This marriage was for one purpose—so they could both be included in the ancient whale expedition to the Diamantina Islands. Yet it was only hours after the wedding and Leah felt indelibly marked. An invisible link existed between them, and Leah doubted that either one of them would ever be the same again.

Carrying a cup of coffee with her, Leah moved into the living room. She sat opposite him and crossed her long legs. "I thought we might talk about the goals of the expedition."

"First tell me something about the ancient whale."

"All right," Leah agreed. "There are about a hundred known species of whales divided into two suborders. The scientific names are Mysticeti and

Odontoceti. Or to say it another way, whalebone whales and toothed whales.''

Cain nodded, his eyes lowered. Leah realized that she was probably giving him more information than he wanted. But it was important that he understood the significance of the discovery of this whale last year.

"Ancient whales," she continued, "are in a third separate category. The reason they're called ancient whales is because it's been presumed for years that they were extinct.''

"What are our chances of photographing one?"

Leah wouldn't be anything but truthful. "Slim, at best.''

"But there will be ample opportunity to view the other species?''

"Definitely. Probably closer than you've ever thought you would get to a whale. There's been a boat supplied and—''

"You're wearing the ring.''

His statement caught her off guard, and her gaze fell to her left hand. "Yes." She didn't elaborate, not sure why she'd relented and slipped it on her finger. "As I was saying about the boat—" she swallowed, suddenly ill at ease "—I'm hoping that we can get—''

"Why?''

"For the photos, of course.''

"I'm asking about the ring. What made you decide to wear it?''

Leah didn't know how to explain something she wasn't sure of herself. "I only hope there's enough time to gather all the material I'll need.''

The room became quiet. "That wasn't what I asked."

Deliberately, she uncrossed her legs and stood. "I think I'll check the oven."

"I'll only follow you."

"I don't know why," she shouted, unreasonably angry that he would demand an answer when she obviously didn't have one. "It was there, and you're right, I'm going to need one. And this will save us the trouble of going out and buying one. Now, are you satisfied?"

The doorbell chimed before Cain had the opportunity to answer.

Leah glared accusingly at the door, marched across the room and turned the handle. "Yes," she said heatedly.

"Darling." Siggy stood on the other side. Shock moved across his eyes. "Is something wrong?" he said gently, reaching for her limp shoulders and bringing her into his embrace. "Of course you're upset. It's about yesterday, isn't it?"

"Siggy."

"No, no. It's my turn. You're right, so right, my love. I was cheating us both by not telling Mother about us. I talked to her this evening and—"

"Siggy, please, let me explain," Leah pleaded as she stepped back out of his arms.

"Mother approves, darling. Do you understand what that means?"

The urge to laugh was almost overwhelming. "Mother approves," Leah echoed.

Cain stood and moved behind Leah, placing a possessive hand on her neck. "Is there a problem?"

Siggy stiffened, then straightened the corner of his bow tie. "Who is this man?" He directed his question to Leah.

"Is there something I can do for you?" Cain answered stiffly. "I'm Leah's husband."

Chapter Three

Leah?" Siggy couldn't have looked more stunned. His eyes rounded and his cheeks puffed out like someone who had come under sudden attack. Slowly he regained his composure enough to continue speaking. "Is this true?"

Frustrated and impatient, Leah glared angrily at Cain. He had no right to adopt this high-handed attitude. From the smug smile that played across his mouth, he was obviously enjoying her fiancé's discomfort. "Siggy, let me explain," Leah pleaded, a thread of despair weaving its way through her voice.

The hand at the base of her neck tightened as Cain drew her possessively closer. "Just answer the question, darling."

"Leah?" Again Siggy's shocked, hurt gaze sought hers. "Is it true?"

"Yes, but there are . . . extenuating circumstances."

The smile Siggy gave her was decidedly dispirited. "There'd have to be. Only yesterday you wanted to be *my* wife."

Her heart leaped with pity at the hurt-little-boy look in his pale-blue eyes.

Siggy took a step in retreat, his shoulders hunching. "Everything would have been all right now that Mother knows. Couldn't you have waited?"

"No, we couldn't." Again Cain had answered for her.

Siggy's gaze skidded from Leah to Cain and then back to her again. Confusion and pain marked his expression. "Then there's nothing left to say. Goodbye, Leah."

"Siggy." The aching sigh of his name must have caused him to hesitate.

"Yes?"

"I'll give you a call in the morning." She ignored the way Cain's fingers were digging into the nape of her neck. "All this can be explained quite simply."

"You won't have time, darling," Cain insisted, his eyes narrowing. "We're both going to be extremely busy from now on."

If possible, Siggy went all the more waxen. A figure of rejection, he turned and walked away, closing the door.

Anger washed over Leah in turbulent waves. The first swells rose quickly to storm intensity, so that she had difficulty forming her thoughts.

"How . . . how dare you!" With a sweep of her hand she slammed the front door closed and turned on Cain like an avenging archangel. Quivers of rage sharpened her voice. The sound of her anger vibrated through the room like a violent ocean storm attacking the shore. This was no squall, but a full-blown tempest.

Even Cain looked shocked at the extent of her wrath. "You can't honestly love that pompous, bureaucratic windbag."

"Why the hell should you care one way or the other? Siggy is part of my life. He had nothing to do with you." To her horror, stinging tears pooled in her eyes, so that Cain swam in and out of focus.

"But he doesn't love you," Cain argued. "Can't you see what he—"

"And you do love me, is that what you're saying? Are you such an expert in love that you know instantly who does and doesn't?" Pride was the only thing that carried her voice now as it quivered and trembled with every word.

"Damn." His gaze narrowed as he plowed a hand through his hair. "You're misinterpreting everything."

"I am?" She gave a weak, hysterical laugh. "Weren't you the one who said I'd be lucky to be any man's wife. Look at me. Do you think I don't know I'm no raving beauty?"

Clearly flustered now, Cain stalked to the other side of the room. "You're not that bad."

"Oh, come now. Be honest. If it hadn't been for this assignment, you wouldn't have given me more than a passing glance."

He gestured indecisively with his hand. "How am I supposed to know that? If it weren't for this assignment we wouldn't have met."

"I'm too tall, too thin and blatantly unattractive. Do you have any idea what that means to someone like me? Siggy cares. For the first time in my life there was a man who looked beyond my face and loved me enough to want to share his life with me. And..." She paused as her voice cracked. "And now, you've done your best to ruin that."

"Leah." He clenched his hands into tight fists. "I apologize. I have no excuse. My behavior was stupid and irrational."

She sniffled and reached for a tissue to blow her nose. "An apology isn't going to reverse what just happened. You may very well have ruined my life."

"All right, all right. Call ... Sidney, and we'll get together and explain everything."

"When?" she demanded.

"Whenever you like."

She reached for the phone, punched out Siggy's number and left a message on his recorder. "He'll return the call," she murmured confidently. Siggy would be willing to clear away any misunderstandings. It didn't matter what Cain Hawkins thought, Leah reminded herself. Siggy loved her and that was the most important thing. When she returned from the Diamantinas her routine could return to normal. Cain would want her out of his life as quickly as possible.

While she was phoning, Cain had gone into the kitchen, and he returned now with a strong cup of coffee. "Here." He set it on the glass coffee table. "Drink this."

The gesture surprised Leah. Cain had already apologized and had promised to make things right between her and Siggy. Now he was thoughtfully taking care of her. "Thank you."

"Do you feel like going over the list of supplies?" He sat across from her and leaned forward as he pulled the tab from his beer can.

Leah waited until he'd taken his first long drink before she answered. "I hope you're not planning to bring that stuff along."

"What?" His gaze followed hers, and a low, husky chuckle escaped. "This, lady, is as essential as film for my camera. Don't worry, I seldom drink more than one or two at a time. Think of it as my brand of cola."

Leah wasn't convinced. If they were going to be spending a lot of time together, alcohol could be a dangerous thing. But the dark gleam in his eye discouraged argument. This was one area where Cain wouldn't compromise. His look confirmed as much.

"Here, take a look at this." He withdrew a pad from his jacket and handed it to Leah.

She glanced over the itemized list of food supplies Cain had typed. The list was extensive and seemed far beyond what they could possibly eat during the course of their trip.

"You've got that look in your eye again," Cain grumbled.

"What look?"

"The one that says you disapprove."

A smile danced across her face, her first since Siggy had come...and gone. "It's just that it seems like so much."

"Perhaps it is, but I'd like to fatten you up a little while we're there."

A small laugh escaped. "My dear Mr. Hawkins, better men than you have tried."

At ease now, Cain chuckled, but the amusement slowly drained from him as his gaze captured hers and the room went still. An expression she couldn't read filtered over his features, an odd mixture of surprise and incredulity. Silence fell between them.

"Is something wrong?" Concerned, Leah wondered what had happened to alter his mood so quickly.

"You're not ugly—or even plain. In fact, you're lovely."

His announcement came out of nowhere. Self-conscious, Leah dropped her gaze to her hands. With the movement, her long hair fell forward, wreathing the delicate features of her oval face. "Don't, please," she whispered entreatingly.

"No, I'm serious. You were laughing just now, and your eyes sparkled, and it struck me: Leah Talmadge is really pretty."

Involuntarily, she flushed. "Cain, I know what I am." In many ways she knew, she was like the Leah from Scripture, the plain, weak-eyed first wife of Jacob. The unloved one.

"And you think I'm making it up?"

No, she knew exactly what he was doing. In his own way, Cain was trying to make up to her for what had happened with Siggy.

"Believe what you want, then. But I didn't imagine what I just saw."

Where only minutes before they had been fiercely arguing, now there was kindness in his words. For a time, it had seemed impossible that they would ever manage to work together. Now Leah had no doubts that they could and would.

"Everything's going to work out fine," Cain said with a confidence that was irrefutable. "Tomorrow we'll meet with Dr. Brewster and your...Sidney. I'm hoping that we'll be ready to leave by the end of the week."

Leah was stunned. "So soon?"

"The faster we're out of here, the better. If we stick around California another week, something else might crop up that could cause a change in plans. Can you be ready?"

"If I can meet a man one day and marry him the next, I can do anything. Lead the way, partner."

"Now you're talking. We're a team; we can't forget that."

The oven timer rang, announcing that their "aluminum meals" were ready. Cain followed her into the kitchen, and while she took them out of the oven, he set the table. Wordlessly, they worked together. What Cain had said was true—they were a team. In the coming weeks they'd be spending a lot of time together. Yesterday the thought had terrified her, but tonight she felt at ease with Cain Hawkins. Their peace would hold because they both wanted this expedition to succeed.

With all that needed to be discussed and planned, Cain didn't leave her apartment until the early-morning hours. She turned the dead bolt lock after he'd gone and leaned wearily against the door. Releasing a soft yawn, she brushed the hair off her face with her hands. Surprisingly, Cain was a meticulous organizer; his expertise was undeniable. The opportunity of a lifetime was opening up for them and her heart swelled with excitement.

Not until Leah had undressed and climbed into bed did the realization come. A chill raced up her spine, and her fingers went cold as they gripped the sheets. Her chest ached with the unexpected pain of it, and she pressed her palm over her heart.

Tonight was her wedding night!

A heavy frown formed deep creases in her brow as Leah's gaze slid to the simple gold band on her ring finger. This so-called marriage was wrong. Her heart had known that from the beginning. The uncertainty she'd experienced as she stood in front of Judge Preston was only a foreshadowing of what was sure to follow.

Slowly Leah lay back and stared at the ceiling. A flip of the lamp switch and the room was cast into instant blackness. The night seemed to press down on Leah. As a teenager, she had often dreamed of her wedding, seeing it as the one day in her life when she was sure to be beautiful. Wearing a long white gown and flowing veil, she would stand before friends and family and give testament to her love. A love that was meant to span a lifetime. Her wedding night would be one of discovery and joy. Not in her cruelest nightmares had she suspected that she would be spending it alone.

Moon shadows flickered across the walls as Leah rolled over, pulled the blankets over her shoulders and took in a shuddering sigh. Even ugly women should be allowed their fantasies. But not Leah. So much for dreams. So much for romance. So much for love.

The relief on Dr. Brewster's wrinkled face was evident in every craggy line. "My children, I couldn't be more pleased." He slapped Cain across the back and shyly kissed Leah's cheek. "I realize that marriage must have sounded a bit drastic, but I can't imagine sending a better team to the islands. Everything will work out splendidly. Just you wait."

"I think it will," Cain agreed.

Perhaps the project would work out well, but as to carelessly linking their lives, Leah wasn't nearly as confident. Their marriage was supposed to be a two-month business arrangement, but the gold band around her finger felt as if it weighed a hundred pounds. Leah knew that when she slipped it from her hand to return to Cain after the expedition, her finger would be indelibly marked by its presence for all her life.

They left Dr. Brewster's office with their travel documents, airline tickets and a list of contacts in Australia and New Zealand.

"Where to from here?" Cain questioned once they'd reached the university parking lot.

With a false smile of courage, Leah lowered her chin fractionally. "I'm having lunch with Siggy."

"You, not us." Cain's voice was clipped and direct. "In that case, I'll drop you off at your apartment." He held the car door open for her, and she gracefully swung her long legs inside.

"It's not that I don't want you to come." She felt obliged to explain, and her soft voice thinned to a quivering note. "But I think it will be a lot better if I see Siggy alone."

"Sure." His gaze seemed to lock on the pulsing vein in her neck, and it was all Leah could do not to turn up her collar. While she stared ahead, unnerved by his sudden interest in her heart rate, Cain started the car and pulled into the heavy traffic in the street.

"Without getting too personal, maybe you can tell me what you find so intriguing about Sidney."

Leah had difficulty disguising her grimace. If Cain called Siggy Sidney one more time, she'd scream. From the first, she'd known his game. He did it on purpose, just to get a rise out of her, and she refused to give him one.

"Well?" Cain prompted. "You were going to marry the guy; certainly you saw something in him."

"Of course I did...do," she corrected hastily. "Siggy's intelligent, sensitive, hardworking."

"From what he said about *Mother*, I'd say he's tied to the apron strings, wouldn't you?"

Leah had despaired over that herself, but there wasn't anything that she and Siggy couldn't settle once they were married. "Siggy has a strong sense of family."

Cain's attention shifted from the slow-paced traffic to her. "Are you always this loyal?" The lines etched about his eyes crinkled as he studied her. But it wasn't a smile he was giving her.

"When you care deeply about someone, then it's only natural to want to defend him."

"Care deeply or love?" Cain demanded.

His question struck a raw nerve. Leah had trouble herself distinguishing between the two when it came to Siggy. She cared about him. She was planning on being his wife. Of course she loved him.

"You can't answer me, can you?"

"I love him." Leah tore the admission through the constricted muscles of her throat. "No woman agrees to be a man's wife if she doesn't love him."

Cain's thick brow arched mockingly. "Oh?" Pointedly, his gaze fell to her ring finger as a mocking reminder that only yesterday she had married him without love or commitment.

For a mutinous moment, Leah wanted to shout at him for being unfair. Instead, she pressed her lips tightly closed and stared out the side window.

They didn't speak again until Cain dropped her off in her parking lot. Leah started to let herself out.

"What time will you be back?" Cain wanted to know.

Leah shrugged noncommittally. "I haven't any idea." At the scowl he was giving her, she added, "Did you need me for something?"

"No." His gaze refused to meet hers. "Enjoy yourself."

The instant Leah closed the car door, Cain sped away, his tires screeching as he pulled out of the parking lot.

Bewildered, Leah watched him go. Cain was acting like a jealous husband. Not that he cared for her himself; he just didn't like the idea of her seeing Siggy. Why, she didn't know. But Cain Hawkins wasn't an easy man to decipher.

Siggy was already seated at their favorite restaurant when Leah arrived. As a vegetarian, Siggy would only dine at a handful of restaurants, even though Leah had often argued that he could order a meatless meal almost anywhere.

"Leah." As she approached the table, he stood and held out a chair for her.

"Hello, Siggy," she murmured self-consciously. "I'm so pleased that you agreed to see me."

"Well, yes, that was rather considerate of me under the circumstances."

Unfolding the napkin gave her something to do with her hands as Leah struggled with her explanation. "Marrying Cain isn't what it seems," she began haltingly. "Cain and I were forced to marry or give up the expedition."

A smile relaxed Siggy's tense features. "I thought as much. I knew you'd never do something like this without good reason. It's not a real marriage, is it? I can't imagine you making love with that unpleasant fellow."

Leah could feel the color flowering in her face. Two bright rosebuds appeared on each cheek and flashed like neon lights for all to witness her embarrassment. "Of course we haven't."

Siggy's chuckle was decidedly relieved. "This is strictly a business arrangement then."

"Yes, strictly business." This entire discussion was humiliating.

"And..." Siggy hesitated, obviously disconcerted. "How shall I put this?"

"I don't plan to ever sleep with him, if that's what you want to know."

Clearing his throat, Siggy flashed her a warm smile. "I had to be sure you weren't going to mix business with pleasure." Finding himself highly amusing, Siggy snorted loudly.

"Siggy," she flashed. "I'm a scientist with a mission. Just because Cain and I will be alone on the island together doesn't mean I'll find him attractive."

"You may be a scientist, my dear, but you're also a woman. A man like Cain Hawkins herds women in unconsciously."

Cain wasn't a ladies' man, Leah knew that much. If anything, he avoided relationships. His camera and his pictures were his life; he didn't need anything else and made a point of saying so.

"Now you're being unfair. Cain's not like that," she said, fighting back the urge to defend him even further.

Siggy's response was a loud cough as he lifted the menu and studied it carefully. Leah wondered why he bothered to read it. He never ordered anything but the zucchini quiche anyway.

The waitress arrived and took their order. True to form, Siggy ordered the quiche; Leah asked for the spinach salad.

Their meals arrived a few minutes later. As Leah dipped her fork into the bowl of greens, an unexpected smile quivered at the corners of her mouth. She knew exactly what Cain would say about this meal. He'd insist that she have pasta on the side and cheesecake for dessert.

Obviously troubled again, Siggy toyed with his meal. "You do plan to divorce the man."

"Of course," Leah returned instantly. "We've agreed to take care of that the first week after we return."

Siggy seemed to breathe easier. "Mother must never know. You understand that, don't you, Leah?"

"I won't say a word," she promised. "It isn't as if it's a real marriage," she went on, "but one of convenience strictly for professional reasons." She couldn't understand why she felt compelled to repeat that. The thought flashed through her mind that she was saying it more for her benefit than Siggy's.

"I understand why you've done this," Siggy continued. "But I can't say I'm pleased. However, trust is vital in any relationship, and I want you to know I trust you implicitly." Having said his piece, Siggy nodded curtly.

"Thank you," Leah murmured, and bowed her head. A ray of light hit the gold band on her finger, causing her to catch her breath softly. This marriage was one of pretense. Deep down in her heart, she doubted Cain Hawkins had it in him to love someone of flesh and blood. His wife was a camera, his children his pictures. Then why, dear God why, did she feel so married?

The Los Angeles airport was crammed with people, all of them in a hurry. A blaring voice over the loudspeaker announced a flight's departure gate, and Leah paused to be sure it wasn't hers. Nerves caused her stomach to knot painfully. Excitement seared through her blood. It had been a test of endurance, but together she and Cain had managed to meet the deadline they'd set for themselves. Barely. Leah was convinced that the first week she was on the island, all she'd be able to do was sleep.

Showing his concern for her well-being, Dr. Brewster had kindly arranged hotel accommodations in Sydney, Australia. From Sydney they would fly directly to Perth and meet with their contact, Hugh Kimo.

"Excited?" Cain's eyes smiled into hers.

"I don't think I can stand it." Her gaze scanned the milling crowd. They'd be boarding any minute, and Siggy had said he'd be there to see her off. That was one thing she could count on: if Siggy said he was going to be someplace, he'd be there. Of all the people Leah had known in her life, Siggy was the most dependable—and predictable.

"Looking for someone?" Cain's mouth was pulled up in a mirthless smile.

He knew exactly whom she was expecting. "I don't understand it; Siggy's never late."

"I hope I didn't inadvertently give him the wrong gate number."

"Cain!" She expelled his name with the cutting edge of anger. Neither man had made any pretense of liking the other, but to have Cain stoop to lying was unfair.

"Leah, Leah, there you are." Breathlessly, Siggy arrived, flustered and obviously relieved to have found her in time. "I've had the most horrible afternoon. This place is a madhouse, and no one seemed to know which gate you were departing from. One would think these airlines would keep better track of these things."

"I suppose your methods would be an improvement," Cain inserted, coming to stand beside Leah. His gaze was hard and disapproving as he made no attempt to disguise his dislike of Siggy.

Apparently not wishing to cause a scene, Siggy ignored Cain and reached inside his jacket pocket for a jeweler's box. He handed it to Leah.

"Siggy," she breathed in surprise.

"Go ahead," he urged, "open it."

Lifting the black lid, Leah discovered a small gold heart and a delicate chain, nestled in a bed of velvet. "Siggy, it's beautiful." Tears stung the back of her eyes. The gesture was so unexpected and so thoughtful that she gently brushed her lips over his cheek, finding no better way to express her appreciation.

Her genuine pleasure caused Siggy to flush with satisfaction. "I want you to wear it while you're away so you won't forget me." He fixed his gaze pointedly on Cain.

"I'd never forget you." She wiped away the first salty tear with the back of her hand. "I don't know how to thank you."

The grim set of Cain's mouth told her that he didn't care for this sentimental exchange. His attitude was difficult to understand. She supposed that in some mysterious way his male pride had been challenged by Siggy, although she couldn't understand why.

Lifting the delicate necklace from its plush bed, Siggy held it up, prepared to help Leah put it on. She turned and lifted her hair as he placed the heart in the hollow of her throat and closed the clasp. Never one to display his affection publicly, Siggy was somewhat clumsy as he turned Leah around and kissed her soundly. The unexpected force of his mouth grinding over hers shocked Leah; his violent embrace knocked the wind from her lungs. Instinctively her hands sought his shoulders to maintain her balance.

Releasing her, Siggy gave Cain a self-satisfied glare. "Don't you so much as touch her," he warned smugly. "Leah's mine."

With a savagely impatient movement, Cain turned and stalked away.

Looking pleased with himself, Siggy stood in front of Leah and placed his hands on her shoulders. "Remember that I'll be waiting for you. Be true, my love, be true."

"You know I will." Lowering her gaze, Leah fought the urge to wipe his kiss from her mouth and was relieved to hear that her flight was now boarding. She had wanted Siggy to come to the airport, but his selfish, brutal kiss had ruined her enjoyment of his unexpected gift. Siggy had come to stake his claim on her so that Cain would know in unconditional terms that she was his. Maybe, after all these months, she should be glad that Siggy was finally showing some signs of possessiveness. But she wasn't.

A quick survey of the area confirmed that Cain had already entered the boarding tunnel without her. Securing the strap of her carry-on bag over her shoulder, Leah offered Siggy a feeble smile.

"I'll call you in two months," she said, eager to be on her way.

Hands in his pants pockets, Siggy gave her his practiced hurt-little-boy look. "Hurry back."

Not goodbye, not good luck, just a reminder that he wanted her to hurry through the most important assignment of her career.

"Goodbye, Siggy." Turning, she handed the stewardess her ticket and headed down the tunnel that led her into the belly of the 747.

Cain was in his assigned seat when Leah joined him. His attention was focused on a magazine taken from the pocket in front of him. After she'd stored her carry-on bag in the compartment above their seats, she joined him.

Their eyes met, and his gaze raked her face, pausing on the swollen fullness of her lips. The look he gave her made her feel unclean.

The silence stretched between them oppressively. Within minutes the huge aircraft was taxiing down the runway. The roar of the engine was deafening as a surge of magnificent power thrust them into the welcoming blue sky.

Still Cain didn't speak, and in agitated reaction, Leah fingered the gold heart at her throat. The movement attracted Cain's attention.

"You must be pleased with yourself," he declared cruelly. "There aren't many unattractive women who can be married to one man and engaged to another."

Leah struggled not to reveal the agony his words had inflicted. "Not many," she agreed, her voice sarcastically low and controlled to disguise the quiver of pain. It cost Leah everything to meet his gaze with a look of haughty indifference. That accomplished, she swiveled her head and closed her eyes under the onslaught of pain. Cain had attacked her where he knew he would inflict the most damage, and he had succeeded beyond anything he would ever realize.

"Leah," he murmured her name forcefully. "Damn it, I didn't mean that."

"Why hedge now? It's true. A girl like me is lucky to have any man want to marry her."

Cain's features hardened. "I didn't mean it." His hand reached for hers and squeezed so hard it almost hurt.

Her eyes blazed for an angry second. "Whether you meant it or not is immaterial. What you said is true." Jerking her hand free from his grasp, she continued to stare out the window, blind to anything but the ache that throbbed in her heart.

The next thing Leah knew, she was being gently shaken awake. "Leah," Cain whispered beside her ear. "Lunch is arriving."

To her acute embarrassment, Leah realized that in her sleep she had used Cain's shoulder as a pillow.

"I would have let you sleep, but I don't want you missing any meals." Her fiery gaze produced a soft chuckle from him. "Now, now, my dear, we're going to spend two months together. There's no call to be testy at the start of our adventure."

Their flight between Los Angeles International Airport and Sydney, Australia, was fourteen hours and spanned two calendar days because they crossed the international date line.

Although Leah slept—or made a pretense of sleeping—almost the entire time, she was exhausted when they touched down in Sydney.

Like a puppet with no will of its own, she followed Cain out of the plane, through customs and into the taxi that delivered them to the hotel.

Not until they were in the lobby, with people bustling around them in a flurry of activity, did Leah acknowledge how drowsy she was. Sitting on the edge of her suitcase, Leah waited while Cain signed the register and murmured something that caused the man at the counter to smile.

"Welcome to Sydney, Mr. and Mrs. Hawkins," the bellhop said in greeting as he held up the key to one room.

Chapter Four

Just what do you think you're doing?'' Leah whispered fiercely while they waited for the elevator. "I insist on having my own room.''

"Leah, darling,'' Cain murmured, smiling beguilingly behind clenched teeth. "Let's not air our dirty laundry in the hotel lobby.''

"I refuse to sleep in the same room with you. Isn't that clear enough, or do I need to shout it?'' She ground out the words angrily, unconcerned if anyone was listening or not. She was tired and crabby, and she didn't want to stand outside an elevator arguing with the infuriating Cain Hawkins.

Whistling, his hands clasped behind his back, the bellhop gave no indication he heard any of her angry tirade, although Leah noticed that he avoided looking directly at her.

The heavy metal doors of the elevator swished open, and pressing a firm hand at the small of her back, Cain escorted Leah inside. "We'll talk about it later," he returned just as insistently. "Not here and not now. Understand?"

With cool haughtiness, Leah stood with her back ramrod straight, counting the orange lights that indicated the floors they were passing. Chancing a glance at Cain as they left the elevator, Leah found that his gaze was opaque, his face schooled to show none of his thoughts. Not so much as a twitch of a nerve or a flicker of an eyelash disclosed his feelings. And yet, she could feel the frustration and anger that exuded from him with every breath.

The bellhop opened the door to the suite and delivered their baggage with an economy of movement, seemingly eager to be on his way as quickly as possible.

Leah offered him an apologetic smile as he hurried past her. With her arms crossed, Leah was determined to stand in the outside hall until Cain acquiesced to her demand to sleep in a room of her own.

"Are you coming in or not?" Cain's eyes sliced into her from the other side of the doorway.

"Not."

"For heaven's sake, be reasonable." Cain's weary frown revealed the extent of his fatigue and the fragile thread that held back his anger. "If you think I'm going to attack you, then rest assured, I'm too damn tired to do anything, and that includes arguing with you."

"It's not unreasonable to want some privacy." She was dangerously close to tears.

"I requested twin beds. That, at least, should please you." A hint of amusement touched his dusky, dark eyes. "I told the hotel clerk that my wife snores."

"There's no way I'm going to spend the night in that room with you," she replied in a taut voice. "And, for your information, I don't snore."

Rubbing a hand over his tired eyes, Cain released an irritated breath and slowly shook his head. "All right, come in and I'll phone the front desk and arrange for another room. You can have this one. I'll move."

"Thank you." But there was no sense of triumph as Leah crossed the threshold into the hotel room.

The suite was surprisingly large, with huge picture windows that granted a spectacular view of Sydney and the harbor below. Leah's eye caught a fleeting glimpse of the renowned Sydney Opera House, and her first impression was that the huge white structure resembled oversized sails billowing with wind.

The twin beds dominated the room and shared a common nightstand where the telephone rested. Cain sat on the edge of the mattress and reached for the phone.

"Leah, for God's sake, won't you reconsider? What if the government official for the Diamantinas hears that we insisted on separate rooms? He may wonder if we're really married."

"I brought a copy of the wedding certificate." She had already anticipated a problem there. "We were married in a civil ceremony and I have the paper that proves it."

"Barely civil, as I recall."

Cain's sarcasm was lost on her. He could throw all the barbs he wished and nothing would affect her. She was simply too tired to care.

The silence became oppressive as Leah lifted her overnight bag onto the top of the mattress and removed the things she needed. Her fingers shook slightly, and she could feel Cain's gaze following her movements, his mouth ominously taut.

Without another word, he called the front desk. She waited until he'd finished before she spoke. "If you'll excuse me, I'd like to freshen up before going to bed." With her nightgown and bathrobe draped over her arm, she paused. "You will be gone before I'm finished?"

His look was filled with angry resentment. "Would it be too much to ask to let me stay here until there's another room available?"

"Of course not. I didn't mean..." Everything was going wrong. She hadn't meant to sound like such a prude, but if he were to see her in the revealing nightgown, he'd know how thin she was, and how flatchested. She might be exhausted, but this was a matter of pride.

"Take your bath," he demanded tightly. "I'll do my best to be out of here."

"Thank you." An odd breathlessness invaded her voice. The door to the bathroom clicked closed, and Leah stood in the middle of the cold tile floor and felt the prickling of tears at the back of her eyes. She prayed the soothing water would dispel the black mood that wrapped itself around her like a cloak of gloom. His heartless words on the plane returned to taunt her. Cain believed she was ugly. She knew that herself, so it shouldn't bother her. But for a minute, just one moment, he had made her believe that she could be beautiful. His cruelty had ruined that and set the record straight.

The water lapping against the edge of the tub had cooled before Leah could summon the energy to climb out of the comforting bath. She took longer than usual drying off in the hopes that Cain would have gone and he wouldn't see her. But if he did, that couldn't be helped, and she was determined to hold her head high and ignore any sarcastic comment. Loosely tying the sash around her narrow waist, she squared her shoulders, mentally preparing herself for the coming assault. She'd known from the beginning how intuitive Cain Hawkins was, but she had only suspected his ruthlessness. Within minutes he had recognized her vulnerability, and he had no compunction against using it to his advantage.

The sun had set, casting the room in hues of pink. As she opened the bathroom door, Leah's gaze was drawn magnetically to the scene outside her window. It reminded her of some of the magnificent sunsets she'd seen in Cain's books—the brilliant golden orb low on the horizon; the silhouettes of a hundred skyscrapers reflected in shades of red. From the scene outside her window, Leah's gaze sought the man who dominated her thoughts. A soft smile touched her eyes as she found him sprawled across the top of the mattress sound asleep. Slumber relaxed the lines of his face and made him seem younger. Unexpectedly, a surge of something akin to tenderness brushed her heart. She admired and respected Cain the photographer, but Cain the man was a dangerous puzzle.

An extra blanket was folded on the shelf in the closet across from the bathroom. Standing on tiptoe, Leah brought it down, then gently laid it over his shoulders.

Standing above him gave her the opportunity to study his face. Relaxed, it had a childlike vulnerability. The deeply etched lines about his eyes showed faded areas where the sun hadn't tanned his skin. His hair needed trimming; it curled upward slightly at the base of his neck. Leah had thought he would cut it before they left California, but clearly she couldn't second-guess Cain. He was his own man and would wear his hair down the middle of his back if he wanted. A lazy smile curved the corners of her mouth. The urge to reach out and touch him was almost irresistible. What she was experiencing, she decided, was a latent maternal instinct.

Leah had just peeled back the sheets to her bed when the phone rang urgently. She grabbed it and whispered into the receiver, not wanting to wake Cain. "Hello?"

"Mrs. Hawkins?"

"Yes..." It was on the tip of her tongue to correct him and explain that her name was Talmadge.

"Your husband requested another room. We have that suite available for him." The clerk sounded friendly and helpful.

"I apologize for any inconvenience, but we won't be needing the extra room."

"That's no problem," the man assured her. "Gud-day."

"Gudday," Leah answered with a tired smile, and replaced the receiver.

A glance at Cain assured her that the phone hadn't awakened him. With the travel alarm set on the stand, Leah slipped her long legs between clean, fresh sheets. Her forearm was tucked under her pillow as she stared across the narrow space that separated her from Cain. Her eyes drifted closed, but she forced them open again, desiring one last look at Cain before she slept. Her last thought before she slid into peaceful surrender was that she was glad he was there.

A sharp clicking noise found its way into her warm dream and Leah winced, irritated to have her fantasy interrupted. She was on the rubber raft off Kahu, the island where they'd be staying, when forty tons of whale broke the surface amid a storm of spray. Excitement caused her heart rate to soar. These marvelous giants of the sea were her greatest love.

The clicking sound returned and was soon followed by another. Grumbling at the intrusion, Leah rolled over, bringing the sheets with her.

"Good morning, lady."

Cain. Her eyes flew open. He was in the room with her, and that awful sound was his camera.

"It's a beautiful morning," he continued, undaunted by her irritated grumble.

She struggled to a sitting position, keeping the blanket under her neck. "What time is it?" she asked, rubbing the weariness from eyes that refused to focus.

"Six." Cain was balanced on the arm of the chair and leaned against the window, snapping pictures of the city below. "Breakfast is on the way," he announced without turning around. "And you're right, you don't snore." He paused and turned to her, his gaze gently examining her face, lingering for a heart-stopping second on her lips. "But you do gurgle."

"I don't either," she snapped.

"Oh." He jumped down from the chair and smiled broadly. "And when was the last time you slept with someone who'd know?"

The quick flow of color into her face caused Leah to cover her hot cheeks with her hands.

Cain's laugh was low and sensuous. "Just as I suspected."

"I should have had you carted out of here." She wasn't up to trading insults with him. Not this early in the morning, when she hadn't had her first cup of coffee.

"You probably should have," he agreed. "But I'm glad you didn't."

"How could I? You were sound asleep by the time I got out of the bath."

"Was I?" Cain teased softly, sitting on the edge of his unmade bed and fiddling with his camera lens.

Leah went cold, then hot. "You mean..." Flashing hazel eyes darted him a fiery glare. So he'd been playing a game with her last night as she stood above him and felt that surge of tenderness. Siggy was right,

Cain Hawkins wasn't to be trusted. Not even for a minute.

A suggestion of controlled amusement was in the slight curl of Cain's upper lip, and her palm itched to slap that awful grin from his face.

"That was a rotten thing to do," she stormed, reaching for her robe at the end of the bed. "You really are unscrupulous. Siggy warned me about you. He said—"

Cain's sword-sharp gaze silenced her immediately and pinned her against the bed. "Listen and listen good, Leah. I won't have lover boy's name tossed at me for the next two months. Yearn for him all you want, but don't mention his name again. Understand?"

The violence with which he spoke shocked her, and she blinked back in surprise. She didn't know why Cain disliked Siggy so much, but it put her in an uncomfortable position. If he didn't want her to mention Siggy, then she wouldn't. But it didn't make sense. Cain stood and crossed the room, his hands stuffed into his pockets. He stood with his back to her, granting her the privacy to climb out of bed. "Breakfast will be here any minute. Maybe you should dress now."

Heeding his advice, Leah fairly flew into the bathroom, dragging her overnight case with her.

The flight between Sydney and Perth took the better part of the day. As a seasoned traveler, Cain didn't seem to be troubled with jet lag, but Leah felt as if she'd been turned inside out. Not only were they eighteen hours ahead of California time, but the seasons were reversed, and what had been lingering autumn days in San Diego had turned into early spring "down under." Dr. Brewster had warned her that it would take several days for her body to adjust, and Leah acknowledged wryly that he was more than right. It didn't seem to matter that she'd had a good night's sleep in Sydney and had slept extensively on the flight from California. She felt a weariness that reached all the way to her bones.

They were met at the airport in Perth by a government official from the Diamantinas. Dressed in a dark business suit, he was tall, with intensely dark eyes.

"Welcome to Perth," he said, shaking Cain's outstretched hand, then doing the same to Leah's. "My name is Hugh Kimo."

Dr. Brewster had mentioned that Hugh would be contacting them in Perth, and would later escort them to Ruaehu, the Diamantinas' capital city.

"My government is most anxious to have your stay in the Diamantinas be profitable to science and to man's understanding of our friends the whales." The formal speech was followed by a warm smile of welcome.

"Thank you," Cain said for them both. "And we're most eager to arrive and begin our study."

Their luggage was beginning to appear on the carousel, and Cain reached for a heavy suitcase.

"First," Hugh continued, "I want to assure you that the supplies you requested have been delivered."

"The dish antenna?" Leah questioned eagerly. The device would be invaluable for recording whale location, especially at night when she would be unable to view their progress from the lookout post hewed out of the rock cliff. In addition to studying migration routes, Leah hoped to investigate the sounds of the whales and their correlation to behavior. But that goal was secondary.

"Yes, the antenna has been installed according to your instructions." Hugh's smile was filled with pride. Leah's happy eyes met Cain's. They were so close now, that she regretted they wouldn't be leaving immediately for the islands. An extra day in Perth would only delay their study. Cain's look revealed that he too was eager.

"How soon can arrangements be made to leave for Ruaehu?" Cain asked. "As you can understand, both Mrs. Hawkins and I are eager to begin our research."

Research! Leah nearly laughed out loud. Cain's camera finger had been itching since before they left the airport. Already he'd taken scores of pictures of Sydney. And they'd only been there overnight.

Hugh Kimo laughed outright. "Dr. Brewster said that he doubted you two would remain in Perth for long. I'll make arrangements for you to fly to Ruaehu in the morning."

Leah was so excited that she had to restrain herself from throwing her arms around Cain's neck. Her goal was only hours away, and a deep sense of unreality remained. This adventure had been a dream for so many months that even now, when she was preparing to arrive, she couldn't believe it was all going to happen. Early tomorrow morning they would fly to the island's capital and leave the same afternoon for the cliff hut.

Cain's arm came around her shoulders and tightened in a brief hug.

"I'll be dropping you off at the hotel. Perhaps we could meet for dinner later?" Hugh Kimo continued. "There remain only a few details we need to discuss."

"We'll look forward to that," Cain assured the tall man.

The hotel was close to the airport, so that the drive was accomplished in only a few minutes. Hugh Kimo didn't come inside, but asked that they meet him in the lobby later that evening.

As the bellhop loaded their luggage onto the cart, Cain smiled down at Leah. Their delicate truce was holding, and she was convinced that maintaining peace between them was as important to Cain as it was to her.

A hand at her elbow, Cain directed her through the large double glass doors and into the hotel lobby. "I'll see about getting connecting rooms this time," he said somewhat dryly.

"I'd appreciate that," she murmured, feeling ridiculous.

Leah's room was connected to Cain's by a common bath. With less than two hours before their dinner date with Hugh, Leah spent the time taking a long, luxurious bath and doing her hair. She felt somewhat guilty to be tying up the bathroom, but other than for a ten-minute shower, Cain assured her he wouldn't be needing it.

Rarely did Leah spend so much time on her appearance. But she reasoned that it would be a long time before she could pamper herself this way again.

Leah's spirits soared at the look Cain gave her when he joined her in her half of the suite. Automatically, he reached for his camera and was snapping pictures before she had a chance to protest. Long ago, Leah had learned to hate the camera. Her mother had claimed that Leah wasn't photogenic and that that was the reason her photos turned out as they did but Leah knew differently. A camera might distort a likeness to some extent, but mirrors didn't lie.

"Don't, please," she begged, casting her gaze down to the carpet.

"What's wrong?" Cain's look was bewildered as he lowered the sophisticated camera.

Turning, Leah made the pretense of checking inside her purse. "I just don't like having my picture taken, that's all."

"Why not?" he asked curtly.

"Because." She hated him for dragging this out.

"That's no reason." He was as determined to find out as she was not to tell him.

"Leah?" A hand at her shoulder turned her around. "Answer me." His enticing, velvet-smooth tone added to her confusion. She kept her eyes centered on the pattern of the carpet, unwilling to meet his gaze.

"Shouldn't we be in the lobby?" Her heart was doing a maddening drum roll that affected her voice so that it trembled softly from her lips.

"Hugh won't be there for another fifteen minutes."

"Please," she begged, hating the crazy weakness that was attacking her knees. His hand that cupped her shoulder seemed to burn through the navy-blue wool dress and sear her sensitive skin. It was unfair that his touch should affect her this way. Her fingers were clenched in front of her, her knuckles white.

"All right, I won't force the issue." He dropped his hand and returned briefly to his room to store the camera.

When he returned, Leah noted that his mouth was curved cynically, adding harshness to his uneven features.

"Are you angry?"

He looked up, surprised. "No, should I be?"

Gently, she shook her head and reached for her room key, which lay on top of the dresser. Forcing her chin up, she offered him a weak smile. "Shall we go?"

Hugh Kimo was waiting for them in the lobby as arranged. His car was just outside the hotel. The restaurant on the beach where he took them specialized in lobster, one of Leah's favorite foods.

Although she joined in the conversation, her gaze drifted constantly to the ocean and the pure white beach. Cain's eyes followed hers, and when their gazes met once, briefly, he smiled, letting her know he thought the scene just as beautiful as she did.

The meal was fantastic, and just when Leah was convinced she couldn't eat another thing, Cain ordered dessert for her.

"Cain," she whispered hotly, doing her best to disguise her anger. Nervously, she smoothed her hand over the white linen napkin on her lap. "Really, I couldn't eat anything more."

"I'm fattening her up," Cain explained with a chuckle to Hugh Kimo.

His laugh infuriated her all the more, and her heart was screaming with frustration. When the chocolate torte was delivered, Leah tilted her chin a fraction of an inch in a gesture of pride. Her murky brown eyes flashed with avenging sparks that told Cain exactly what he could do with his high-handed methods.

Shaking his head in mock disgust, Cain reached over and took the dessert and ate it himself.

Leah was surprised when Cain suggested that he and Leah would return to the hotel by taxi. Outside the restaurant, they shook hands with their host and agreed upon a time to meet in the morning, then watched as Hugh drove away.

"You don't mind, do you?" Cain asked, casually draping his arm across her shoulder. "A walk along the beach will do us both good."

"I'd like that." She forgot about being angry over the dessert. Having lived in southern California all these years, Leah was ashamed to admit that the only time she had been to the beach was for her work.

She didn't protest when Cain's arm moved to her waist. As he'd mentioned several times, they were a team. And if she was honest, she'd admit that she enjoyed being linked with Cain.

A crescent moon lit their way down the flawless beach. Sand sank deep into her pumps, and Leah paused to slip her shoes from her feet, loving the feel of the cool, damp sand.

"Tomorrow night we'll be on the island," Cain spoke, his voice coated with eagerness.

"I've waited so long for this." She recalled how excited she'd been when Dr. Brewster first considered her for this assignment. And later, how thrilled she'd felt when she learned that the world-famous photographer Cain Hawkins would be coming with her. Little had she dreamed that she would be accompanying him as his wife.

They walked so far that the lights of the restaurant behind them looked like fireflies on a summer's eve.

"Cold?" Cain's deep voice was disturbingly close to her ear.

"No," Leah breathed with difficulty. Cain was pressed much closer to her side than necessary. The large male hand at her waist had slid up so that it rested just beneath her breast. Unbidden, unwanted, the thought came to her, and she wondered insanely what it would be like if Cain were to caress her breasts. Would their smallness disappoint him? A shudder of longing shook her.

"You are cold." Cain sounded almost angry as he released her and yanked his jacket from his arms to place it over her shoulders.

Humiliating color flowed into her face, and she lowered her gaze, afraid he would read the desire in her eyes.

"Are you warmer now?" he asked. His hands remained at her neck.

"Yes . . . yes." Her voice was low and throbbing.

"Leah." His finger under her chin raised her eyes to his. "What's wrong?"

Desperately she shook her head. A bubble of apprehension was lodged in her throat; she doubted she could have spoken if her life depended on it.

"Leah." Her name was a whispered caress. In the dim light of the moon, he lowered his mouth to hers in a feather-light kiss that lasted but an instant.

Closing her eyes to the delicious sensations that wrapped themselves around her, she swayed toward him slightly.

Hands at her shoulders, Cain paused and waited as if he expected her to reject him. But she couldn't. Not when for days she'd really been wanting him to kiss her. Not when she yearned for the feel of his body close to hers. Not when the man holding her was her husband.

His hands eased up from her shoulders to the smooth line of her jaw, directing her face upward to meet the hungry descent of his mouth. With a small sigh of surrender, she parted her lips, eager to experience the depth and passion of his kiss.

Cain's mouth was on hers, hard and compelling, kissing her with a fierceness that stole her breath and rocked her to the core of her being. Again and again his mouth sought hers until her arms slid convulsively around his neck and she clung to him. Her fingers ruffled through the thick growth of his dark hair, loving the feel of it.

Cain's hands fell from her face to her breasts in a gentle butterfly caress, lingering over them until her nipples quivered and throbbed through the wool dress.

"Leah?" He was asking so much with just the sound of her name. He wanted her. Now. Here. On the sand. And she hadn't the will to refuse him.

"I need you," he whispered urgently against her lips. He seemed to want her to tell him how much she needed him. But she couldn't. The only sounds that passed from her lips were small, weak cries of longing. She had never felt anything this strong and overpowering.

"Tell me you want me." His voice was a hoarse whisper as he ordered her to answer him. His hands were driving her to the limit of her endurance as they roamed her back and buttocks, arching her against his hard body, his need abundantly evident.

Still she couldn't; words were impossible as she struggled to speak. Cain buried his face in the gentle curve of her neck, kissing her hungrily.

Suddenly, abruptly, he stopped, and with a tortured sigh, he pushed himself away.

Bereft, Leah was left to face the cold, her shoulders heaving with shock. "What's wrong? Oh, Cain," she whimpered, "what did I do wrong?" Her heart was pounding so hard she thought she would die of longing. Her whole body was burning with need.

Cain was taking in deep breaths of air, fighting for control.

"Cain, please." She blinked, still not comprehending what had happened.

Without a word, Cain reached out a hand and lifted the small gold heart that was nestled in the hollow of her throat. The heart Siggy had given to her.

"I promised that I'd send you back pure as the driven snow to that bastard. And I intend to keep my word." He let the heart drop back against her skin.

Instinctively her hand reached for the heart, her fingers nervously toying with it.

"As long as you continue to wear that necklace, I won't touch you. Understand?"

Tears of humiliation scalded her cheeks as she shook her head, telling him that she did.

"Then let's get back to the hotel. We have a big day tomorrow. We'll need a good night's sleep."

But neither of them got one. Back at their suite in their separate rooms, they both lay awake, thinking of each other.

The fierce wind bobbed the motorboat like a toy upon the rough waves.

"There's a storm coming," Hugh Kimo shouted trying to be heard above the roar of the wind and sea. "I'm afraid I won't be able to stay on the island long."

"Don't worry. Once our things have been unloaded, there isn't any reason for you to stay."

Hugh looked relieved and nodded appreciatively.

The spray from a large wave splashed against Leah's face, and she wiped the moisture aside. No longer was she able to keep watch ahead as the wind and sea tossed their craft at will.

Everything had been going smoothly as they crossed the five miles of water that separated the main island from the smaller one of Kahu. The squall had come on quickly and without warning.

Suddenly a cloud burst overhead and thick drops of rain began pounding at them from every side. Someone handed Leah a slicker to protect her from the downpour. She slipped her arms into sleeves that were miles too long.

The motorboat hit the sandy beach with a heavy thud, and Leah was jerked forward unexpectedly. Cain's arm prevented her from slamming into the side of the boat. She tried to thank him, but the wind carried her voice in the opposite direction.

Once they were beached, there was a flurry of activity as the boat was unloaded and the luggage carried up the rickety stairs that led to the cliff house. Leah stayed at the boat to make sure nothing was left behind.

"The radio..." Hugh began haltingly.

"Yes...yes." Cain nodded sharply. "I've worked one before. Don't worry, I'll take care of everything. Go while you've got the chance." He waited until Hugh and his men were back inside the boat before pushing against the side of it, guiding it back into the water.

Leah returned Hugh's hand signal. They had arrived and were safe.

Cain didn't try to speak as he helped her up the wooden stairs built into the steep cliff. Leah was panting when they reached the top, and she paused for a moment to catch her breath.

The heavy wooden door to the hut was open, their luggage set just inside. Leah and Cain stumbled into the large room. The area to her left would serve as their kitchen. An old black stove and a small table were set against one wall. To the right was a much larger table stacked high with the equipment they had requested. Two doors led off from the main room.

Stripping the wet coat from her arms, Leah moved into the place she would call home for two long months.

Cain closed the door, blocking out the fierce sound of the wind. "That was quite a welcome," he murmured, removing his drenched jacket.

"I'm hoping this storm moves out as fast as it came."

"It should." But Cain didn't sound overly confident.

Now that they had arrived, their work was only beginning. Lifting a suitcase, Leah moved to carry it toward the bedroom.

Cain stopped her, his large frame blocking the door. "Before you go in there, I think I should tell you there's a small problem."

Her searching gaze sought his. "What?"

As Cain swung open the door, Leah felt a sinking feeling attack her stomach. The room—indeed, the entire hut—contained only one bed. A double one.

Chapter Five

I assumed...I thought..." Leah stuttered, feeling the blood drain from her face, leaving her waxen and unnaturally pale. In the past week they'd nearly worked themselves to exhaustion to meet their self-imposed schedule. The sleeping arrangements hadn't crossed Leah's mind. Not once. How incredibly stupid she'd been.

"I take it you don't want to share the bed?" Cain mocked lightly.

"Absolutely not. I don't even want you in the same room." Crossing her arms to ward off a sudden chill, Leah paced the compact area that comprised their living quarters.

Doing a quick survey of their stark quarters, her eyes gleamed with satisfaction. "That table would work." She pointed to the one stacked with boxes at the other end of the room.

"As a bed?" Cain looked shocked. "Leah, that table is meant to be used as a desk. We're going to need it. Be reasonable, will you?"

"So what's to say we can't clear it off every night? You don't have to do it, I will," she volunteered, her voice sharp and vigorous. "It'll be my responsibility."

"Are you offering to sleep there as well?" Cain cut in sarcastically. "Because I have no intention of doing so. I have work to do, and there's no way in hell I'm sleeping on a narrow table to satisfy your perverted sense of modesty."

"All right, I don't blame you. I'll sleep there." Her fingers closed tightly over the back of the chair until she feared her nails would snap. "I don't mind. Really."

The scowl darkening Cain's features revealed what he thought of the idea. But the shrug he gave her was indifferent. "If that's what you want, feel free."

The storm grew in intensity; a demon wind howled outside until Leah was sure the small dwelling would be torn from its foundation. The storm in her heart raged with the same intensity. This situation was quickly going from bad to worse and she didn't need it. Of course Cain wanted to share the bed—and probably whatever else he could take. He didn't have anything to lose. But Leah wasn't fool enough to believe that once they returned to California it would make a difference. Without a care, without a thought, Cain would be on his way to the next adventure, to another assignment. After all, that was their agreement.

Her mind buzzing, Leah inspected the supplies she'd requested. Cain lit a fire in the cast-iron stove that would serve as a means of cooking and as their only source of heat.

"Where's the bathroom?" she asked shyly after a while. "I like to freshen up before dinner."

"Bathroom?" He cocked his brow in sarcastic amusement. "If you mean the outhouse, it's outside and fifty yards to your left."

Embarrassed, Leah spun around, hot color reddening her cheeks.

"Leah, this isn't exactly the Hilton. Didn't you stop to think about the living arrangements?"

Perhaps it was stupid not to have considered the more mundane aspects of this expedition, but this cliff house hadn't entered her thoughts once. She wasn't here to vacation. "No," she admitted somewhat defensively. "There was so much else to consider that the living arrangements didn't enter..." Flustered now, she wiped a hand across her face. "I came to study the whales."

"And I came to take their pictures." His words were a subtle reminder that he wasn't on Kahu to steal her virginity. When she didn't respond, he turned his back to her. "I'll cook tonight and you can do the honors tomorrow."

"Fine."

Determined to make her plan work, Leah stepped to the table. She'd sleep there and make the best of it. Several boxes were stacked on top of each other, and

Leah realized it would be a monumental task to unpack and assemble them tonight. Already she was tired, the effects of jet lag having hit her with as much impact as the storm.

While Cain worked silently in the kitchen area, Leah feverishly took down the boxes, examined their contents and set them aside. Most of the equipment, the telescopes and recorders, would be used exclusively by Leah. Since many of the tools she'd requested had to be run with batteries, she would need to conserve power.

The dim light cast from the two lanterns was barely enough to work by, and before she was halfway finished, it became necessary to move one closer.

"Dinner's ready," Cain announced.

"I'm too busy right now."

A disgusted sound of exasperation came from him. "I don't give a damn. You're eating now."

If he made so much as one wisecrack about how she couldn't afford to skip meals, Leah was determined to dump his dinner over the top of Cain's arrogant head.

"In a minute."

"Now, Leah!" Cain repeated his demand. A muscle twitched warningly along the side of his jaw.

"Oh, all right," she conceded ungraciously, knowing it would be useless to argue. There would be far more serious matters to expend her energies on later. Like the matter of the bed.

They ate in silence, and afterward Leah washed the dishes, using water heated by the stove. Not until she'd finished did she realize that the storm outside had abated. Unfortunately, the one in her heart continued to rage.

"It's late," Cain announced without preamble.

He didn't need to remind her; she felt bone weary. "You go to bed.... I'll make do out here."

The deep-grooved lines beside his mouth went white. "Have it your way. There's a soft mattress in there or a hard, cold tabletop out here."

"I know," she replied miserably. The crazy part was that if she were shapely and beautiful, she wouldn't have minded nearly so much. Logic had nothing to do with it. Cain felt no constraint when commenting on her looks and figure. Long ago she had come to terms with her plainness, but at the same time Cain's remarks had the power to cause her pain. Every thoughtless word he uttered seemed to slice her to the bone. With Cain out of the room, Leah examined the gold band on her ring finger. This single piece of gold Cain had placed on her finger had somehow allotted him the power to inflict emotional pain. Leah could toss aside thoughtless, cruel words from other men. But not from Cain.

Carrying an armload of blankets, Cain returned to set them on top of the table. He hesitated. "Leah," he breathed slowly, carefully choosing words. "I swore I wouldn't touch you as long as you continued to wear... what's his name's... heart."

Unconsciously she reached for the necklace, rubbing the gold trinket between two fingers.

Her actions produced a heavy scowl from Cain. "We're here alone. Trust is essential. I promised not to touch you, and I keep my word."

Holding a thick wool blanket against her stomach, Leah cast her gaze to the plain wood floor. "I...prefer to stay out here." In some ways Leah was more afraid of her response to Cain than any fear that he would take her against her will.

Cain threw up his hands. "Have it your way, then." He returned to the bedroom and left the door ajar.

Mumbling under her breath, admitting she was a fool, Leah spread out a couple of blankets for padding on the table's hard surface. With the pillow in place, she climbed on top and spread the warm wool blanket over her. The first thing she readily acknowledged was how incredibly unyielding a table was. And dressed in jeans and a sweater wasn't exactly conducive to a good night's sleep either. Lying on her side with her forearm tucked under the feather pillow, she leaned over and turned off the lantern. The hut became pitch-black, so dark that a shiver of nervous apprehension raced up her spine.

"Good night," Cain called out, and she cursed him silently for sounding so comfortable.

"Good night," Leah returned, forcing a cheerful, happy note into her voice. After everything else she'd gone through to come to this island, a tabletop for a bed was something she could do without.

Ten minutes later, her own bones causing her the most discomfort, Leah rolled over. The wool blanket fell to the floor. "Damn," she muttered impatiently, and reached for it. To her horror her whole body slid off the table, and with a frightened cry she landed with a loud thump on the cold, hard floor.

"What happened?" Cain shouted.

Although she couldn't see him in the dark, she knew from the direction of his voice that he was standing in the doorway of the bedroom.

"Nothing, I . . . I fell off the table, that's all."

"Are you okay?"

He didn't need to sound so smug, she fumed. "Fine," she answered, doing her best to sound just as amused.

Situated atop her makeshift bed once again, Leah forced her eyes closed and did her utmost to fall asleep. An hour later, cuddled in a tight ball to keep warm, she rolled over and, to her horror, tumbled off the side of the table again. Landing with a jarring thud, she was too stunned to move. Her breath came in uneven gasps of hurt and anger. Tears stung the back of her eyes.

"That does it." The unrestrained fury in Cain's voice tightened the muscles of her stomach. "Damn it, Leah, I've had it."

"I'm fine...I just fell...again, that's all." Her voice thinned to a quivering note as she heard Cain storm into the room.

"Where's the lantern?" he shouted at her. Before she could answer, he crashed into a cardboard box, knocking it over. His angry cry of pain filled the room as the contents of the crate spilled onto the floor.

Struggling to a standing position, Leah blindly reached out for him. Her groping arm came in contact with the solid wall of his chest. "Are you hurt?"

"No, but I'm damn mad. You're coming into that bed before your stubbornness kills us both."

"I won't."

Cain snorted.

"I won't," she repeated.

Cain said nothing, but an arm looped around her waist and lifted her off the floor. Against his superior strength her weak struggles were a futile effort.

The next thing Leah knew she was falling through space to land on a soft cushion of comfort and warmth. A hand on each shoulder held her in place. "Now listen, and listen good," Cain spoke with infuriating calm. "You're sleeping here tonight and so am I. To soothe the outraged virgin in you, I'll remain outside the covers. Understand?"

"Yes." Her soft voice was pitifully weak.

He released her and pulled back the thick layer of blankets. "Get in."

Wordlessly she did as he demanded, feeling incredibly small and stupid.

Once she was in place, he lowered his weight beside her and rolled over so that she was presented with a clear view of his back. Within minutes his even breathing assured Leah he was asleep. Soon after that she fell into an uneasy slumber.

And so their adventure began. The first week was spent unloading and setting up the monitoring equipment. In this area, Cain was an invaluable aid. At night, exhausted, they fell into bed, Leah under the covers, Cain curled up with a wool blanket on top of them. And every morning, to her utter embarrassment, Leah woke with her arms wrapped around Cain's lean ribs, her head pillowed by his broad chest.

Drawn by his warmth and comforted by his arms, she came to him naturally in her sleep.

Waking first, Leah would slip from his loose hold, praying that he would never be the wiser. If he was aware of the way she unconsciously reached for him, he never spoke of it. For that, Leah would be eternally grateful. She found the situation embarrassing in the extreme.

The sixth day after their landing, Leah spotted her first whales. She'd discovered that, although the telescopes allowed her to view miles of water, it was easier to stand and look over the rolling waves of the Indian Ocean using her field glasses.

The vast, dark shapes resembled huge black submarines. As the massive forty-ton creatures came closer to shore and into her view, Leah realized that these were the first in the large family of right whales, southern right whales, a once-abundant species that was now among the rarest.

"Cain," she screamed, pointing toward the lolling creatures. "They're here."

Standing on the beach far below, Cain shielded his eyes from the sun to study the swelling seas. Turning, he signaled that he'd be right up. In record time he was at her side.

"Holy Moses, look at those babies." Crouched down behind his camera, Cain began working at a furious speed. The clicking noise was repeated so fast that the sound blended to a low hum. "Humpbacks, right?"

"No." Laughing, Leah shook her head. "Southern rights."

"Right? That's not any kind of name for a whale."

"The sailors of old named them that because they were the right ones to hunt," Leah explained. "They float after death and can easily be towed to shore or butchered at sea." She winced as she explained, hating the thought of any of these lovely, graceful creatures dying such a brutal death at the hands of man.

The entire afternoon was spent watching the herds frolic close to shore. Cain was in photographer's heaven, carrying cameras and equipment between the beach and Leah's perch on the cliff top.

Now that the first herds were arriving, Leah wanted to secure the sonar equipment in place. In the morning they would take out the motorized rubber raft and anchor three transmitters. The underwater microphones suspended from them would catch the whales' sounds.

In the evening, when Cain radioed his report to Hugh Kimo in Ruaehu, he asked Hugh to send up a spotter plane in the morning to report the whales' course.

"What's all this sonar equipment going to tell you?" Cain asked as she finished with the evening dishes.

Leaning a hip against the enamel sink, Leah wiped the last plate clean with a dishcloth, her hands continuing to rub in a circular motion long after the plate was dry. "Several things. First, I don't need to keep my eyes peeled on the ocean or count on the Cessna to know when they're coming. And second, I'm hoping to monitor and record the whale sounds. Later, when

I'm back at the university, I'll study the sound waves to see if I can further decipher their meaning.''

"Like breaking a code?"

"Exactly." She smiled, pleased at his interest. "Oh, Cain, this is so exciting I can hardly stand it." Her heart swelled with joy.

Gingerly, she put the plate aside and set the kettle back on the stove to heat. "Coffee?"

"Please." Cain delivered his cup to her, coming to stand at her side. His intensely dark eyes studied her, narrowing slightly. The last time he'd looked at her that way had been in California, when he'd told her she was lovely. Her cheeks warmed with rising color, and she glanced away.

"It's been quite a day," she murmured as a means of breaking the uneasy silence. When she did look up, it was a mistake; she recognized it immediately. The warmth and nearness of his body were distractions she couldn't ignore.

Those wonderful, intense eyes were fixed on her moist lips. Leah couldn't stop staring at him. Nervously, her fingers tightened around the empty mug. His gaze was bright and glittering, his desire evident with every breath he drew. A mere inch separated them, and Leah could see every line in his sun-bronzed face, every pore, every lash. His mouth, hard and straight, was silently beckoning her to come taste the pleasure of his kiss.

A surge of longing raged through her, and Leah shuddered slightly. Cain saw it and his nostrils flared. Their eyes were locked in a silent battle of wills. He wanted her to come to him, to make the first move.

She couldn't. How much better it would be if Cain had never kissed her, had never shown her the marvels of his touch. For today, this minute, he filled her senses. But reality was only weeks away, and she couldn't allow the beauty of this island, of this time, to sway her.

Every beat of her heart was demanding that she step into his arms, but somehow, somewhere deep inside a strength she didn't know she possessed came to her rescue and she resisted.

"You said you wanted coffee?"

"Yes, I did."

Her hand shook as she poured him a cup. Cain took it and returned to the desk, sitting with his back to her.

Several hours later, Leah pretended she was asleep when Cain came to bed. Her back was to him as he eased his weight onto the soft mattress and stretched out beside her. Leah didn't know how any two people could be so close and yet have the whole universe stretch between them.

The wind whipped Leah's long blond hair about her face as the rubber raft skipped across the top of the waves. A feeling of exhilaration caused her heart to soar. Behind her, in the rear of the raft, Cain sat beside the motor.

Leah planned to place the sonar equipment in a huge triangle, each underwater microphone separated by half a mile. Earlier, Hugh had radioed the location of approaching whale pods, and it was now their job to get the equipment in place before the whales arrived.

They had just finished placing the third and final orange buoy in the swelling water when Cain pointed to a huge shape in the distance. Leah turned just in time to see the great right whale hurl itself out of the water. The huge mammal was as black as a raven's wing and as sleek as silk. It hit the ocean surface with a boom that sounded like a World War II cannon. Water sprayed in every direction, and although they were a safe distance, a few drops managed to wet them.

Cain, with his ever-ready camera, took a series of shots and beamed her a brilliant smile, giving her the thumbs-up signal. The triumph, however, soon drained from Cain's eyes to be replaced with a wary light. "He's coming our way. Should I try to outrun him?"

"We can't." Leah's heart moved to her throat as the creature, fifty feet long and weighing at least a ton for every foot, approached and circled their rubber craft. "Cut the engine," Leah cried.

Cain did as she asked, but his look was skeptical.

"She may have a calf in the area and just wants to check us out to be sure we mean her no harm." Although Leah wouldn't admit it, she was frightened. Their rubber raft could be easily overturned, and with all the equipment Cain insisted on keeping around his neck, he'd sink straight to the bottom. Mentally, Leah chided herself for her crazy thoughts. They were about to become whale fodder, and she was worried that Cain wouldn't be able to stay afloat.

"Would it help if I promise to touch up her photo—you know, hide a few of those extra pounds?"

Before Leah could respond, the whale turned its tail flukes and swished the raft strongly from side to side, with Leah and Cain clinging for their lives. Leah held on to the edges in a death grip, closing her eyes to the terror that strangled her throat muscles. Their small raft was tossed about like a trembling leaf caught in an autumn windstorm.

A cry of pure terror froze in her lungs as the mammoth creature, tired of its game, backed up and, with its giant flukes, lifted the rubber raft, Cain and Leah inside, about six inches off the water's surface.

Tense, every cell, every muscle alert, Leah began to shake violently. Panic wouldn't allow her to breathe, and when she did, the air rasped painfully in her throat. Finally a noise penetrated her dulled senses: a clicking sound, followed by another and another, with whispered phrases of ''Wow, fantastic, unbelievable.''

Their lives were balancing precariously on the whim of a fifty-ton whale and Cain was taking pictures.

The rubber raft hung in the air for the longest minute of Leah's life; then the whale slowly, with the utmost control, lowered its flukes and deliberately set them back on the water unscathed.

Leah released a sigh of relief and tasted the blood in her mouth, unaware that all the while she'd been viciously biting her own lip.

For the first time Leah spotted two young calves who loafed nearby. Cain saw them at precisely the same moment as Leah, and again she heard a long series of clicks. More pictures.

The gargantuan creature circled the raft twice more before rejoining her young and swimming away.

"That had to be the most fantastic adventure of my life," Cain called, his voice heavy with excitement. "You won't believe the shots I got."

Leah couldn't believe that he could be that unaffected. She had faced a watery grave with Cain at her side and worried about his safety. All he'd thought about were his precious pictures.

Leah was silent until they reached the shore. Doing her best to restrain the growing anger, she wordlessly helped him secure the raft. His eyes burned over her questioningly, but Leah paid no attention. Her only desire was to be away from him as soon as possible.

"Leah," Cain called to her as she raced up the wooden stairs, but again she ignored him.

When he arrived at the hut, Leah was pacing the floor, her arms crossed, her knuckles clenched. She stopped and glared at him with all the fury of her pounding heart.

Standing just inside the door, Cain regarded her grimly. "All right, let's have it. What's wrong?"

Her arm swung out as she pointed toward the ocean. "We could have been killed out there." Even speaking was difficult as the words crowded on her tongue and escaped on a giant rush of anger.

"Come on, Leah, that mama was just protecting her young. She gave us a warning, that's all."

His calm only served to fuel her fury. "And you loved it."

"You're this angry because I wasn't scared?"

"Are you so incredibly stupid that you don't know the destruction those whales are capable of? Our lives were in jeopardy."

"I wasn't unconcerned," he flared.

"You could have fooled me."

What really angered Leah was that her thoughts had been on Cain. Her fears had been more for him than for herself. Whirling, she stormed into the kitchen area and made herself some lunch. Taking the sandwich with her, Leah picked up her gear and headed toward her observation point on the cliff top.

Cain looked stunned for a minute. "Where's my lunch?"

"Take a picture of mine and eat that," she shouted.

Leah didn't make it out the door. Cain's hand snaked out and gripped her arm, brutally hauling her against him. "Damn it, Leah, you're not making any sense."

Her shoulders heaved as she forcefully pushed herself free. "I should have known that you'd be more concerned about your stomach. That fits right in with your character."

"Would you be serious."

"It's difficult to talk to a man whose hair is practically as long as my own."

Cain regarded her sharply, his eyes narrowed and confused. "My hair? We're arguing about my hair? For heaven's sake, woman, be real."

"You know what your problem is, Cain Hawkins? You don't care. Nothing in this world or the next is more important than those pictures you take. Not relationships. Not family. Nothing." Her sarcastic gaze blazed across his face. "The irony of it all is that you hide behind a lens and reveal your soul."

Cain clamped his mouth shut, but his eyes glinted dangerously.

"But once the camera is gone, there's only this...this...love child left over from the sixties. A man who takes pride at shouting to the world that he doesn't care."

"Who the hell gave you the right to dictate how I should live?"

"No one," Leah admitted dryly, and bit her lip to hold back her invective. Cain was incapable of understanding what had upset her. Care and consideration were beyond a man like Cain Hawkins. Everything today had been her fault. She'd allowed herself to get too close to Cain emotionally, allowed herself to care. Well, no more. He could rot and she wouldn't lift a finger to aid him.

He smiled, but his expression was decidedly unpleasant. "Go sit on your perch, Queen Leah, and when you've worked everything out in that twisted, irrational mind of yours, then maybe we can talk."

She scooted past him, but not before she was gifted with a hard, taunting smile and a verbal jab of his own. "If you want to bring up the subject of hair, then maybe you should consider cutting your own."

Leah usually wore her long blond hair tied back at the base of her neck. But today, her hair had somehow worked itself free during their ordeal with the whale. The long stringy strands hung limp and lifeless across her cheek.

"You're right," she muttered, dumping her lunch and binoculars in his arms. "You're absolutely right." Charging across the room, she flung open a drawer and took out a large pair of scissors.

"Leah?" Cain gasped. "I didn't mean—"

"Maybe not, but I did." Tilting her head to the side, she grabbed a handful of her hair and chopped away. Six inches fell to the floor. She quirked her head in the opposite direction and lopped off another handful, letting it fall heedlessly away. Her bangs followed next.

"Leah, for heaven's sake stop," Cain shouted, and the horror in his voice made her look at the cold, hard floor now covered with a thick layer of golden hair. Shaken, Leah cupped her mouth as tears burned her eyes. The first drops scalded her cheeks as she recognized what she had done.

"Cain, oh, Cain." She raised stricken eyes to him and lifted a tentative hand to the side of her head. The clump her fingers investigated prompted a racking sob.

At her side, Cain removed the scissors from her numb fingers.

In her anger, she'd lashed out at him and ended up hurting herself even more. Her hair, her lovely golden hair, was the only beautiful asset she possessed. And now that, too, was ruined. Every breath became a sob.

Very gently, Cain put his arms around her and held her as if he would never let her go. At first she shrugged, resisting his touch, but he would have none of it, holding her fast in his strong arms.

She cried then in earnest, great heaving sobs for caring so much and for hurting just as much because he didn't.

His kiss was at her temple, offering her the comfort she craved. Of their own volition, her arms slid around his waist, molding her slight frame to him, seeking his warmth.

Cain's healing lips found her eyes as he kissed aside each fresh tear. Unable to bear another moment of this sweet torture, Leah tilted back her head so that her lips sought his first. Trembling, her mouth stroked his in a caress so light that it was tantalizing torment.

With a muted groan, Cain ravaged her lips as if he were starving for the taste of them. Leah met his urgent hunger with her own, winding her arms around his neck, her head thrown back under the force of his kiss.

Again and again he kissed her until he shuddered and left the sweetness of her lips to slide his mouth across one cheek. "Dear Lord, Leah."

"I was so scared," she wept. "I thought the whale would kill us, and all you cared about were your pictures."

"I'm sorry, love," he breathed into her ear. "So sorry."

"Hold me," she pleaded. "Just hold me." Her whole body trembled.

"Always," he promised. "Always."

Chapter Six

Taking a step backward, Cain cocked his head to study his handiwork. A pair of scissors dangled from his index finger as he positioned Leah's head first one way and then another before nodding slowly and smiling. "It doesn't look half bad, even if I do say so myself."

Tentatively, her fingers investigated the blunt cut, expecting to find gouges and nicks. Instead, her fingertips brushed against her exposed ear. With a rising sense of dread, she let her hand fall lifelessly to her lap. "It's horrible."

"The least you can do is look," Cain chastised, and gave her a small hand mirror.

Her reflection revealed incredibly sad eyes, red and glistening from recently shed tears. Her full lips were slightly swollen and tender from the heat of Cain's kisses. And her hair, her once-lovely long hair, was gone, replaced with short choppy curls. The sides were styled above her ears and then neatly tapered to the base of her neck. Leah couldn't remember the last time her hair had been this short—probably grade school. To his credit, Cain had done an admirable job of softening the butchered effect resulting from her craziness.

He was right; her hair didn't look bad, but it wasn't her. The stranger whose face flashed back from the mirror was someone else. Siggy wouldn't know this woman, and upon her return she'd be forced to deal with his disapproval. Siggy had always loved her long hair.

"Well?" Cain waited for her approval.

"You did the best you could."

"Leah, you look fine. I mean it."

Standing, she brushed the blond hair from her shoulders and lap. The ache in her heart was heavy as she reached for the broom and swept up the remnants of what once had been her greatest asset. Never had she done anything so foolhardy. She'd behaved like a crazy woman, lashing out at Cain, and then destroying the one part of herself that was beautiful.

Replacing the broom, she gave him a feeble smile. "I'd better get back outside." She retrieved the equipment, then paused in the doorway. "Thank you, Cain."

"Any time." He let her go without an argument, for which she was grateful.

To Leah's surprise, the afternoon passed quickly as she charted her finds and recorded the various sounds of the whales on the battery-powered recorder. The sun was settling from an azure sky into a pink horizon when Cain reappeared. Usually he spent part of the afternoon with her, but today he'd granted her some badly needed privacy and she was grateful.

"How'd it go?" He stood at her side on the cliff top, gazing over the long stretch of rolling waves that crashed onto the virgin shore below. Silently he slipped his arm around her shoulder.

"I saw my first southern blue." Despite the despair that had wrapped itself around her only hours earlier, Leah's voice rose with enthusiasm. "It was magnificent."

"You say that every time," he teased.

"This time it's different. Blue whales are the largest creatures ever to inhabit the earth."

Cain's gaze was skeptical. "Larger than the dinosaurs?"

"Yup."

"You're kidding?" He looked genuinely surprised.

Laughing, she shook her head and slipped her arm around his waist. "I'm not. The largest whale ever recorded was a female blue that measured over a hundred and thirteen feet and weighed about a hundred and seventy tons."

"Wow." The hand that cupped her shoulder tightened, bringing her even closer to his side.

"To put that into perspective, that one blue whale weighed the equivalent of thirty-five elephants or more than two thousand humans." Having him hold her like this, linking herself to him, was flirting with danger, and Leah knew it. But his arms helped ease the ache in her heart, and she couldn't resist this small comfort.

"If you're trying to impress me, you just did."

"Good." Their eyes met, and by unspoken agreement they turned and sauntered lazily toward the hut.

"Now it's my turn to impress you," Cain murmured, his voice an intimate caress against the sensitive skin of her neck.

"Oh?" Quivers of awareness raced down her arms. It cost her the earth to remain stoic. "And just how do you plan to do that?"

"Wait and see."

Leah didn't have to wonder long. When they reached the hut, Cain swung open the door, allowing Leah to step inside first. A flash of unexpected color captured her attention, and Leah gave a small cry of pleasure. In the center of the small wooden table was a handful of wildflowers. White, blue and yellow blossoms stood proudly in an empty beer bottle that served as a vase.

"Oh, Cain, they're lovely." No man had ever given her flowers before, and happiness surged through her. These simple wildflowers were more precious to her than exotic orchids.

His eyes crinkled with a smile at her obvious pleasure. "I read somewhere once that flowers are supposed to lift a woman's spirits."

"Thank you." Impulsively her lips brushed his cheek. "They're lovely."

"There's a method to my madness." He straightened and held out the chair for her. A half smile touched his hard mouth. "After dinner I want you to cut my hair. And when you do, I want to make sure you're in a happy mood.''

Leah raised stricken eyes to him. ''I can't cut your hair. Good grief, look what I did to my own.''

''I took that into consideration.''

Shock receded into astonishment. ''You're serious, aren't you?''

''As far as I'm concerned, we have a deal. I cut your hair; now it's my turn.''

''But—''

''It should have been trimmed weeks ago.''

Leah opened her mouth to argue, but his look discouraged further discussion. She wasn't sure she could do as he asked, but clearly Cain wasn't going to let her out of it.

The meal, succulent white fish sautéed in a delicate wine sauce, was another surprise. Cain had spent the entire afternoon doing little things to lift her spirits. Not only had he hiked across the island in search of wildflowers, but he'd gone fishing. Leah loved him for it because she knew he'd much rather have been out with his camera.

When the table was cleared, Leah dried her damp palms on her thighs as Cain held out the scissors.

''You're sure?'' she questioned for the tenth time in as many minutes.

''Leah!''

''All right, all right.'' He sat in the chair, and Leah draped a towel over his shoulders, using a clothespin to hold it together. Stepping back, she tilted her head to one side and bit into her bottom lip, unsure where she should begin. She chose the back of his head so he wouldn't see how badly her hands were shaking.

The comb brought the disobedient locks to order, and she ran her hand over his crown and down to his nape. The first snip would be the worst. His dark, silky hair curled over her finger. Holding her breath, she cut. She didn't take much, just enough to keep the length above his shirt collar. The dark strands fell to his shoulders and littered the floor. More confident now, Leah moved from his left side to his right, trying to keep the lengths evenly matched.

Content with her progress, Leah moved to stand in front of him as she considered the best way to trim the crown of his head and the loose hair that fell haphazardly across his forehead. Cain seemed constantly to be brushing it aside.

"Well?" he teased. "You're looking at me as if you've seen my picture in the post office. Let me assure you, I'm not on the FBI's most-wanted list."

Not the FBI's list, but certainly on hers. The thought struck her dumb. She did want Cain. Siggy seemed a million miles away, and the necklace she wore felt like an albatross around her neck.

"Leah?" His hand reached for her waist. "Are you okay?"

"I'm fine." She forced a smile and ran her fingers through the hair at the top of his head, pretending she knew what she was doing. The gesture gave her time to align her wandering thoughts. Cain had made his position clear; giving him her heart would only complicate an already complex situation.

"Are you going to finish this or not?" he demanded irritably, beginning to squirm like a five-year-old. "I hate sitting still."

"All right, all right." She used the comb to lift the first locks and snipped carefully, fearful of cutting too much. As she worked, she inched closer and closer. Not until Cain's labored breathing disturbed her concentration did she realize that her breasts were directly in his line of vision. Abruptly, she stopped cutting as the color blossomed in her cheeks. Her treacherous nipples hardened, outlined by the thin cotton material of her T-shirt. She tried to ignore the obvious and concentrate on cutting his hair, but every move made her all the more aware of how intimate it was to stand so close to him. When she lifted her arms higher, her pebble-hard nipples brushed Cain's cheek, and he breathed in harshly and shifted to pull back from her.

Leah felt her face go ten shades of pink, but as hard as she tried she couldn't tame her body's response to him. His warm breath fanned her breasts until her nipples throbbed and swelled. Leah closed her eyes to the onslaught of foreign sensations that rushed over her with an intensity that made her knees go weak.

"That's enough." Abruptly Cain gripped her waist and pushed her back so he could stand. They faced one another, Cain unnaturally pale, the grooves bracketing his mouth white with barely restrained frustration.

Leah knew that her reddened cheeks were as bright as a lighthouse lamp. Surely Cain didn't think she'd purposely tried to seduce him.

Impatiently, he jerked the towel from his shoulders and tossed it on the table. "I'm going out for a while," he mumbled gruffly, and was gone before Leah could reorient herself.

She was reading when Cain returned an hour later. Or at least she made a pretense of being caught up in the book, hiding her face behind the large volume to disguise her uneasiness. Cain apparently didn't feel all that comfortable either, and ten minutes after his return he made an excuse and went to bed.

Leah waited until she was certain he was asleep before joining him. His body was turned away from hers, his back rigid. The mattress dipped as she slid under the blankets. Feeling more self-conscious than ever about their sleeping arrangements, Leah rolled onto her side and forced her eyes closed. It was a long time before she slid into peaceful slumber.

The early-morning light stirred her awake, and unconsciously she turned over, automatically seeking the comforting warmth of Cain's back. When she realized what she was doing, she jerked back. With a small gasp, she sat upright, surprised to find Cain's side of the bed empty.

The coffeepot on the stove was full, and a note propped up on the wooden table told her that he was going to the other side of the island and not to expect him back before late afternoon.

She crumpled up his brief message and tossed it inside the wrought-iron stove to burn. The coward! What did he think she was going to do, play Salome and entice him to her bed? Damn, he already was in her bed.

Dressing in washed-out jeans and an old sweat-shirt, Leah was determined to make herself as unattractive as possible. To her deepest regret, that didn't take much doing.

By the time she'd positioned herself at the lookout perch, her temper had cooled. Within minutes, she was once again content with her world. Placing the earphones over her head, Leah recorded what she was sure was the courting ritual between two whales. The squeaky, high-pitched vibrations grew fainter and fainter as the whales headed south, but the simple message stirred a breath of excitement. A brief smile touched her eyes as she imagined Cain's look if she were to sing such a blatant song for him.

Later, she decided with a chuckle, she'd play back the tape for Cain and see what he thought. No! If she suggested that these sounds were a courting ritual, he could misinterpret her motives.

At noon, Leah spotted the largest pod she'd seen since the first whales arrived. She was so busy documenting their numbers and route that she didn't break for lunch. When she glanced at her watch again it was past four. It didn't make sense to break for lunch now when dinner was only a few hours away.

Cain reappeared sometime after six. Not wanting to appear overanxious for his company, Leah did little more than acknowledge his wave. Mud caked his shoes and pants, and she wondered what adventures he'd gotten himself into today.

"I'm going in to wash up," he shouted as he threw open the door of the hut.

In other words, she was to give him a few minutes of privacy. Not that she minded. There were several things she wanted to do yet this afternoon. Damn, she'd missed him! As much as she hated admitting it, Cain's active involvement with her work had cemented a bond between them. The hours they had spent together in the sun were her most pleasant times on the island.

Leah was kneeling down, collecting her equipment, when the gentle breeze carried the sharp sound of the hut door slamming closed. She tossed a look over her shoulder and was shocked to see Cain's angry strides devouring the distance separating them. His fists were knotted at his sides, his hard features twisted with disdain. Leah couldn't imagine what she'd done to displease him.

Not allowing his anger to intimidate her, she rolled to her feet and brushed the sand and grit from her jeans. Squaring her shoulders, she met his fiery gaze with an outward calm.

"When was the last time you ate?" he demanded.

Leah cringed inwardly. Not that again! From the moment they'd arrived on the island, Cain had appointed himself her nutritionist. He cooked breakfast every morning and sat at the table with her until she'd finished eating. Although they divided the lunch duties, Cain insisted that she eat whether she was hungry or not. Rather than argue, Leah complied.

Her shrug of indifference only flamed his fury. "Damn it, Leah, I am sick of having to baby-sit you."

The facade of indifference evaporated, and Leah flashed him a look as cold and brittle as an Arctic wind. Hurt and anger swelled up inside her. From the moment they'd stepped foot on this island, Leah had more than carried her share. "Baby-sit me!"

"What else do you call it when I'm forced to spoon-feed you three times a day?"

"I don't need a guardian," she snapped.

His face turned to hard, cold stone and filled with such intense anger that it frightened her. There was no reasoning with him, she told herself, and she wouldn't try again. He'd twist her words to suit his anger. It wouldn't do any good to provoke him. And, admittedly, part of her couldn't help cowering from the savage fury in his eyes.

He stormed away, descending the stairs to the beach far below, leaving Leah stunned and shaking. Her legs felt like rubber, and she sank to her knees in the sand. Although she made an effort to refocus her attention on her duties, she discovered she couldn't. Her hands shook, and she pressed her cool palms against her hot cheeks.

Cain didn't reappear until dinner was on the table. Without a word, he pulled out his chair and started eating, attacking his meat with a savagery that really was directed at her.

"The beef's already dead; there's no need to rekill it," Leah chided him.

Cain's jaw tightened ominously, and he shoved his plate aside and stalked into the bedroom. It struck Leah how ludicrous this whole situation was. If Cain weren't so serious, she'd have laughed.

Days stretched into weeks, and Cain acted as if he were on the island alone. It was as though he couldn't tolerate being around her. Leah didn't know what she'd done that was so terrible, but after a while she gave up trying to guess. When she spoke to him, he snapped one-word replies. What he did with his time, she could only guess. He disappeared in the morning and returned late in the afternoon.

At night they would lie side by side, not speaking, barely moving, the sound of their breathing filling the strained silence. She was convinced that if Cain edged any closer to the side of the bed, he'd fall off.

Leah felt trapped in a maze with no exit. She was thoroughly confused and bewildered by his actions. The afternoon she'd cut his hair, Cain had seemed profoundly affected by what had happened. He'd wanted her. She wasn't so naive and inexperienced that she didn't recognize that. Yet, he had rejected her and hadn't treated her the same since. Whatever it was that was troubling Cain had destroyed their friendship.

Leah's fingers toyed idly with the gold heart hanging from her neck. She missed Cain's friendship, missed sharing her findings about the whales. She'd been lonely and hurt these past weeks. Part of her longed to reach out and touch him, yet she couldn't, and a sadness seemed to press heavily on her chest.

Her dreams that night were heavy and dark. She was on the rubber raft alone, pulling up the sonar equipment while Cain stood watching from the beach. Out of nowhere came the blue whale. Its huge flukes rose out of the sea and slammed into the ocean surface, flooding the small raft. Leah clung for her life. Frantically she cried out for Cain to help her, but he was intent on taking her picture and ignored her pleas. Trapped on the surging waves, Leah was tossed into the dark depths of the ocean. Water closed over her, but she clawed her way to the surface. Saltwater filled her mouth and eyes, and she gagged as she fought for every breath. She was drowning while Cain emotionlessly documented her demise.

"Leah . . . Leah." Cain's voice was a soothing purr in her ear.

He'd come! He wasn't going to let her drown.

"Leah." A hand on each shoulder shook her gently. "Wake up."

Her heart pounded as her chest rose and fell dramatically with every hoarse breath. Panic-stricken, Leah clenched his shirt, still trying to save herself from the terrifying depths.

"Leah," Cain's voice rasped close to her ear. "It's only a dream."

A dream. Dazed, she stared at him with eyes that refused to focus. She was going to live. The raft, the whale, the frantic fight for her life had all been a figment of some horrible nightmare. Relief coursed through her as she sagged against the bed and relaxed her death grip on Cain's shirt.

"Are you all right?" he asked in a rough whisper.

She lifted her gaze to his and nodded. The constricting muscles in her throat made speech impossible. Tears shimmered in her eyes and spilled down the side of her face.

Gently, Cain wiped them aside, his callused thumb slightly abrasive against the softness of her cheek. "None of it was real," he murmured.

She nodded, still unable to formulate words. Cain parted his lips as though he wanted to say more, then reconsidered. His mouth hovered above hers, their breaths merging, and she knew he was going to kiss her. His hands roved from her cheeks to cup her ears, tilting her head to receive his burning kiss. But neither moved. A soft, choppy breath shuddered through her as she flattened her palms against his chest, feeling the wild hammering of his heart. Cain groaned and rolled onto his back.

Together they lay side by side, not speaking, not moving, hardly breathing.

"Would it help if I apologized?" she whispered, not chancing a glance at him.

"For a dream?" he scoffed, and some of the old anger crept into his voice.

"No," she murmured, and her lashes fluttered closed as she swallowed her pride. "I want to apologize for whatever I did that made you so angry."

"Leah," he groaned, and rolled onto his side, propping his head up with the palm of one hand. Tenderly, he brushed the short blond curls from her temple. "You didn't do anything."

"Then why?" She turned her head so that she could read the answer in his eyes.

In response, Cain lifted the delicate gold chain from the hollow of her throat, winding it around his index finger until Leah feared it would snap. His brow knit as his grip relaxed. "I made a promise to you in Perth, and with God as my witness, I mean to keep it."

"But?"

"But being with you twenty-four hours a day is making it damn difficult."

Using her elbow as leverage, Leah raised herself, wishing she wasn't so affected by his nearness. "I didn't mean...for that to happen...when I was cutting your hair." Embarrassment caused her voice to quiver, and she lowered her gaze, not wanting him to see how much the incident had stirred her as well.

Cain chuckled lightly and her heart melted. "Do you think I don't know that?"

Leah lowered her head to the feather pillow and released a deep sigh. "I've missed you."

"Me too, lady."

He seldom called her that anymore. In the beginning it had been a minor source of irritation to Leah. But tonight, in the distant light of the moon, it sounded very much like a lover's caress.

"Friends?" she whispered.

For a moment, a furrow of concentration darkened his brow. "Friends," he finally agreed.

The reluctance in his voice dimmed the brilliant light of joy that had shone so brightly just seconds before. "Good night," Leah mumbled, rolling onto her side so that her back was to him.

"Good night," he repeated a moment later, drawing his words out slowly.

The tense silence was back, and Leah forced her eyes closed, wondering if things could ever be the same between them again.

Leah felt the weight on the bed shift as Cain turned toward her, slipping his arm around her middle. His hold was firm but gentle.

"We'll talk in the morning," he promised.

"Yes," she breathed, and a tremulous smile touched her mouth.

Again Cain was gone when Leah woke in the morning, and she wanted to cry with frustration. Hadn't last night meant anything to him? He'd promised they'd talk this morning, and instead he'd run like a rabbit bent on escape. Well, he couldn't avoid her forever.

She quickly donned her mauve cords and a thick cableknit sweater. The leaden gray skies promised a storm, and the room was cold. She was further surprised that the stove hadn't been lit and the coffee wasn't made.

After tucking her feet into tennis shoes, Leah moved outside to investigate.

"Cain."

Her call went unanswered.

Wandering to the edge of the cliff, she buried her hands in her pockets and looked out over the crashing surf. The sight below made her knees go weak and trapped the breath in her lungs.

Cain was in the rubber raft, the angry seas tossing it about like a toy boat. Without warning, a humpback hurled itself from the water and slammed back onto the surface with a thunderous roar.

Leah gave a cry of alarm and covered her mouth in horror. The tiny raft rocked with the impact.

Soon Leah realized it wasn't just one humpback, but a pod of eight feeding from a rich underwater pasture of krill. Like graceful dolphins, they leaped from the ocean bed, their cavernous maws open and spanning thirteen feet.

Amid the humpbacks, oblivious to any danger, was Cain, snapping pictures as fast as his fingers would allow.

Chapter Seven

Leah was pacing the beach when Cain landed the craft. His face was flushed with exhilaration as he pulled the raft onto the shore and hurried toward her, his feet kicking up sand.

"You idiot," she stormed, her eyes burning with a smoldering light. "You unmitigated idiot. What in the hell did you think you were doing?"

"Did you see them? Eight humpbacks feeding cooperatively. It was like a riotous pack of school kids." Oblivious to her fear and anger, he continued to describe what he'd managed to document with his camera. "They launched themselves out of the water like they were bouncing off trampolines. Those pictures were the opportunity of a lifetime."

"Is your life worth so little? Are your pictures that important?" Leah was so frustrated that her voice throbbed. She was shaken to the core of her being, frightened out of her mind for him. And he hadn't even acknowledged the danger.

"Leah," he pleaded, gripping her by the shoulders. "Don't be angry. These pictures are going to impress the world."

"But you could have been killed." She stuffed her trembling hands into her pants pockets and hung her head, reluctant to reveal the tears that clouded her vision. "But I wasn't," he cried exultantly. "Dear Lord, I can't wait to show these shots to my editor."

Once again he had taken his life in his hands with nary a thought. What would she do if anything happened to Cain? Her life wouldn't be worth living.

Draping an arm over her shoulder, Cain led her to the rickety weatherworn stairs built against the cliff wall. "Let's have coffee and I'll tell you all about it."

Leah raised the angle of her chin several degrees, not wanting him to know how much his adventure had terrified her, nor the reasons for her deep-seated fear. With a wry twist of her mouth, she decided that it would serve no useful purpose for Cain to know she loved him.

Back at the hut, hugging a steaming cup of coffee in her hands, Leah listened to Cain talk nonstop for an hour. He'd awakened early, before the first light of dawn, and wandered outside. The thunderous commotion coming from the ocean was what had drawn him to the cliff. The sight of the humpbacks had caused him to run for his camera, and there hadn't been time to wake her. Or at least that was what he said. Leah knew better. Cain must have realized an argument would have ensued had he told her his plans, so he'd left her behind to discover his absence later.

As if he wanted to make it up to her, Cain spent the day at her side, using the telescope while she documented migration patterns and routes.

They chatted about inconsequential details, afraid to speak of the matters that were prominent in their minds.

"Once we're back, how long will it take you to develop the film?" Leah wanted to know, sitting beside him in the grassy brush at the cliff's edge. What she was really asking was how long he'd stay in California before moving on.

"Not long."

Leah blanched. That answered that: Cain wouldn't stay a moment longer than necessary. "I suppose you'll be anxious to get these pictures to your editor."

He hesitated for a moment. "He'll be anxious to see them."

"Of course."

He didn't mention the divorce, although it was paramount in both their minds. Three weeks was all the time that they had left together. A sad smile touched her troubled eyes. Three weeks. It seemed decades too long and a lifetime too short.

The morning air was cool and scented by the fresh breeze coming off the ocean. A shiver danced up her arm, and Leah didn't know if the chill came from without, or within. She'd never forget this moment: Cain was at her side, his look tender, his smile so warm it seemed capable of melting her heart. Her spirit soared like a kite racing toward the heavens. Yet as free as she felt this moment, she knew the reality, the string that controlled her flight.

To distract her bewildered thoughts, she plugged in the recorder and slipped the earphones over her head. The faint sounds being transmitted were ones she didn't recognize: deep, mournful sounds unlike the high-pitched squeaks she normally cataloged. Leah thought they sounded like a funeral dirge.

Lifting her binoculars, Leah studied the ocean to see if she could identify the source of the distress signal she'd overheard.

Two humpbacks, possibly from the same pod that Cain had seen in the morning, were lagging behind the rest of the pod. A mother and her young calf swam side by side. Although it was difficult to determine its age, the calf didn't look more than a few months old.

"Cain," she murmured, slipping off the headphones, "listen to this and tell me what you think."

He eyed her curiously, and then did as she'd requested. His brow creased into thick folds of concentration. Slowly he shook his head. "A mother and her calf?" He arched his brows in question.

Leah nodded, handing him the binoculars as well.

"I don't know," Cain admitted soberly a few moments later. "What do you think's wrong?"

"I'm not exactly sure." All her textbook knowledge wasn't a help to her now. "I'd say it has something to do with that calf of hers." A dark glow of uncertainty entered her hazel eyes.

Turning off the recorder, Leah stood, preparing to deliver her equipment to the hut and pick up what she'd need from inside. "I'm going to take the raft out and investigate."

"Like hell." Cain bounded to his feet like a rocket, his eyes shooting hot sparks. "You can't go out there. The humpback's first instinct will be to protect her calf."

"But I want to help her," Leah argued.

"You get within ten feet of that calf and the mother will come right for you. You wouldn't have a chance."

"I'm not going near the calf."

"The calf's by the mother." His piercing gaze and sarcastic tone shredded her faulty reasoning.

Leah's fingers tightened into a fist. "In other words, it's perfectly fine for you to take a risk, but not me."

"You're damn right. I'm the man."

Seething, Leah closed her eyes to the rising surge of anger. How any man could be so unreasonable, she didn't know. "I'm going out there to help that whale," she stated flatly, brooking no argument.

Cain mockingly inclined his head toward the beach. "And I'd like to see you try." An unnatural smile curved his mouth, and his dark eyes glittered with challenge.

Undeterred, Leah squared her shoulders and with long, purpose-filled strides headed back to the hut.

Cain was blocking the doorway when she reappeared, her rain gear draped over her forearm. "If you think I'm letting you out of here, then you can think again." There were overtones of mocking laughter in his voice that provoked her all the more.

Crossing her arms over her chest, Leah unflinchingly met his gaze. "I'm the scientist here."

"And I'm the one with common sense."

"Ha!" Leah scoffed. "This morning your life was hanging by a thread because you wanted a fistful of snapshots. So don't think you can dictate to me." Not two inches separated them as she came to the doorway of the hut. His outstretched arms prevented her from proceeding.

"Cain, please." Leah's words were filled with anxiety and urgency. Her fists were clenched at her sides. "I'm losing precious time."

A muscle leaped along the line of his jaw and captured her attention. Her gaze strayed down the tanned column of his throat to the unbuttoned front of his shirt. The smooth muscles of his chest gleamed like those of a statue. Leah scolded herself for being affected by his virility. This wasn't the time to notice these things about Cain. Not when she had a mission to accomplish.

Cain hesitated, seeming to measure his words. "I'm asking you as your husband not to go."

Leah's jaw sagged with surprise. The fact that they were married had never been mentioned, never discussed. Yes, they were bound to each other, but not in the normal sense. That he would use that form of persuasion with her now was unscrupulous and unfair.

The flash of resentment from her narrowed eyes must have convinced him of that.

"Leah," he whispered enticingly. His hands gripped her shoulders, keeping her at arm's length. "If you're so concerned, I'll contact Hugh by radio and have him send someone out."

"Whoever came wouldn't be able to do anything more than I could."

Cain held her gaze for a long moment, looking deep into her hazel eyes. What he saw there, she didn't know.

"I'm sorry," he muttered, tightening his grip on her shoulders, his gaze narrow and menacing. "I won't let you go."

"Cain." The breathless tremor in her voice betrayed her frustration. "Please." Her eyes were shimmering with the powerful desire to aid the distressed whale.

Leah felt Cain's resolve weaken as he slowly shook his head. "Damn it, Leah, can't you see what you're sailing into?" His face turned grim, and white lines formed around his tight mouth. "If you're going out, then I'm going with you."

Leah's pulse leaped wildly. He was conceding even when he felt she was wrong, but he wasn't letting her go alone. Her lips curved into a faint smile. "Thank you," she whispered, knowing what it had cost him to bow to her wishes.

He dropped his arms and moved across the room to where his rain gear was stored in the corner of the hut.

"Hurry," she pleaded, "they may have already moved on."

Together they ran to the edge of the cliff to descend the wobbly stairs. The rubber raft was high on the beach, where Cain had left it earlier that morning.

Abruptly, Cain stopped running. His hand gripped Leah's elbow as he pointed toward the spot where the two humpbacks had been sighted.

"What's wrong?"

"They're swimming closer to the shore."

Leah's heart sank, and she felt an oppressive weight settle onto her chest. The humpbacks' direction meant only one thing. "She's dying," Leah whispered.

The fifty-foot humpback came within a stone's throw of the beach. The calf remained close by his mother's side, swimming around her in tight circles. It was apparent that whatever had caused the mother's illness was not afflicting the child. Leah and Cain stood by helplessly; all they could do was watch.

By evening the mother was dead and the mewling sound of her son could be heard up and down the beach. Two days later, the calf was so weak that he didn't protest when Leah got into the water with him. Swimming at his side, using a snorkel and goggles, she could do little more than let him become accustomed to her presence.

With Hugh Kimo's assistance, Leah attempted to feed the young calf enriched milk using a hot water bottle, rubber tubing and a five-gallon drum. Hugh made the trip to the island daily, bringing in large quantities of the formula, but it all ended up in the sea. Leah spent hours coaxing the calf to eat. Cain did what he could to help, holding her makeshift device.

"Leah," he groaned, standing in the surf. "It's not going to work. Give it up before you collapse."

"No," she refused stubbornly. "Come on, Jonah, eat. Please eat."

A half hour later, shaking with cold, miserable in body and spirit, Leah abandoned the effort and walked out of the ocean.

Cain draped a thick towel over her shoulders and set her down in front of a warm fire he'd built on the sand. He sat behind her so that she could lean her back against him and be comforted by his warmth. With his arms wrapped around her, he brushed the wet strands of hair from her face. Numb with cold, and utterly discouraged, she battled back tears of exhaustion.

"I want him to live so much," she whispered.

"I know, love."

The affectionate term barely registered. "He's just a baby. He needs his mother."

"I know."

Completely drained of energy, Leah closed her eyes and fell into a deep, dreamless sleep. Lying side by side in front of the fire, Cain and Leah slept on the beach. Leah woke at dawn, her arms and legs entwined with Cain's. Her first thought was of Jonah, and she rushed to the water's edge. Jonah was alive, but for how much longer she couldn't know.

That morning, using the rubber raft, Cain hauled the decaying mother out to another part of the island. On close inspection, Leah was amazed at how heavily encrusted with seaweed, worms and crustaceans, especially barnacles, the humpback was, but she doubted that any of this had contributed to her demise.

When Hugh arrived later that same morning, he brought another specialist with him from the Diamantinas to aid Leah with the autopsy. The postmortem revealed that a liver ailment had caused the mother's death. Antibiotics were administered to the three-month-old Jonah, although the calf showed no signs of the mother's sickness. After an hour's struggle, the four managed to get the young whale to accept the rich, creamy formula, but the young calf was nervous and objected strenuously to all these humans fussing over him. Only Leah would the young mammal accept at his side.

Five days later, Jonah gave up eating, and Leah realized it would only be a few days before he joined his mother.

Death was just a matter of time, but Leah refused to allow her friend to die without her at his side. She spent several hours every day in the water, swimming at the calf's side, stroking the top and sides of his head, doing what little she could to encourage him.

Other humpbacks passed, and Leah came to enjoy their sporty nature. She smiled at their antics and was amazed to see that they sometimes scratched themselves against the rocks. When Cain asked her about two whales that he saw smacking each other with their flippers, she explained that this was part of their mating ritual. The sounds could be heard up to a mile away.

In the evenings, Cain built a fire on the beach so that Leah could warm herself when she came out of the water. The flames flickered invitingly as he stood ready with a towel to dry her.

Miserably cold and defeated in spirit, Leah welcomed the iron band of his arms as he draped a thick towel over her shoulders.

"How much longer can he hold on?" Cain whispered, leading her to a blanket spread out in front of the warm fire that crackled with dry wood.

"Soon. Not more than a couple of days," she answered, holding back the tears.

No one would have guessed that Jonah would hold
on to life as long as he had. For two weeks, Leah had
expected him to die, and for two weeks he had held on,
growing weaker, less and less responsive.

Leah was at Jonah's side the following morning
when he died. She shed tears, grateful that she had
been there with him, and continued patting his head
long after he'd stopped breathing. Only when all her
tears of sadness had been shed did she come out from
the water. Cain met her on the shore and held her tight
in his arms. Willingly Leah accepted his comfort.

Once she was warm and dry and sitting at the
kitchen table with a hot cup of soup in front of her,
Cain radioed the news to Hugh, who promised to return the following day.

For the second time in as many weeks, Cain hauled
the corpse of a humpback whale out to sea.

An incredible sadness filled Leah as she watched
Jonah being towed away. She stood on the beach,
holding back the tears until Hugh, Cain and Jonah
were out of sight. Her arms cuddled her stomach as
she tried to beat down the emotion. Staring sight-
lessly ahead, she closed her eyes and fought back a
sob, but still tears flowed from the corners of her eyes
and down the sides of her face.

By the time Cain returned, Leah had composed
herself and was busy at the duties she had neglected
while working with Jonah. Cain had kept a log of the

passing whales, and she spent the afternoon reviewing his brief notes.

When dusk arrived to purple the sky, Leah paused from her position at the lookout over the Indian Ocean and sighed sadly. In a few days, less than a week now, they would be leaving the island, and this magical adventure would be at an end. Once in California, she and Cain would separate and there would be only her memories to remind her of this enchanted time.

Even Cain noted her mood that evening as they readied for bed. The entire time Leah was working with the young calf, she had slept on the beach, Cain at her side. He had cuddled her close, spoon fashion, his arm draped protectively over her waist. He'd warmed her with his body and comforted her with his quiet concern. He'd brought her meals, but didn't force her to eat. He'd spoken soothingly to her when she was too cold and weak to answer. He'd held her, encouraged her and cared for her. Leah never stopped to question Cain's gentleness during that time. He was there. She needed him and she didn't analyze his motives. If the situation had been reversed, she would have done the same for him. There wasn't any reason to read something more into his actions.

"You've been quiet tonight," he murmured as they lay side by side in the darkened room.

Leah's fingers gripped the sheet. "I haven't been good company lately. I apologize for that."

His hand reached for hers and squeezed it gently. "There's no need to feel sorry. You were busy." His thumb made lazy, circling motions at the inside of her wrist. A warm, tingling sensation was creeping up her arm. He was so close, she could smell the fresh scent of the sea mingled with the faint smell of hard work and the spicy after-shave he'd used that morning.

"After the past two weeks, I'm willing to promise never to take the raft out in a pod of humpbacks if you promise not to risk your health by nursing a sick whale."

Leah bit into her lower lip and nodded. She'd so desperately wanted Jonah to live. She'd have done anything to help him. Fresh tears burned for release, and she inhaled a shuddering breath. "Okay," was all she could manage.

Cain rolled to face her and wiped the tear that had started down her cheek. "Don't cry." The words were filled with a warm tenderness that she'd never thought to hear from this man who cared only for his work.

"I'm sorry," she sniffled, rolling away from him. It was bad enough that he was witness to this display of weakness and emotion. She couldn't stand to face him.

"Leah," he moaned her name, and tugged gently at her shoulder, easing her onto her back. "Don't block me out. Let me hold you."

With a weak cry, she did as he asked, reaching for him in the dark. Her arms went around his neck as she buried her tear-streaked face in his throat.

Half sitting, half lying, Cain tightened his arms around her. One arm was draped across the small of her back while the other hand stroked her head.

"I wanted him to live," she moaned.

"I know. I wanted him to live, too." The words
were so soft, so tender that Leah lifted her red, blotchy
face to him and smiled tentatively. She didn't speak,
although her heart was bursting with a thousand
things she realized she could never say. Her eyes filled
again, but these tears weren't for the loss of the young
whale. They were the tears of a virgin wife who would
never know her husband's love.

Cain shifted their positions so that she was lying flat
on the mattress and he was bending over her. His finger wiped the moisture from her face and paused to
skim her tear-moistened lips. His gaze locked with hers
in the golden rays of a disinterested moon.

Leah felt the small shudder that went all the way
through him. She knew before he dipped his head that
he was going to kiss her. This was a time predestined,
a kiss ordained, and her heart pounded erratically in
eager anticipation.

At first his mouth merely touched hers, as if he
expected her to push him away. Leah didn't move. He
retreated, bringing his head back so that he could gaze
into her eyes. Willingly she met his look and gave him
a weak, trembling smile of encouragement.

He groaned her name, and his mouth moved closer
to hers until their breaths mingled. He was a scant half
inch from her when he paused. Her mind reeled crazily, demanding that he give her what she craved. How
could he come so close and deny her? Deny them
both? A weak cry of protest slipped from her parted
lips. Cain ignored her pleas. Her hands tightened their
grasp at the nape of his neck to force his head down.
He resisted. Timidly she arched her back so that her

unrestrained breasts rubbed his naked torso, shooting hot waves of desire through her blood. Her nipples hardened, and he groaned as she pressed herself intimately closer. Yet he wouldn't yield and grant her the kiss.

No longer demure, no longer shy, Leah brought her mouth to his and outlined his bottom lip with the dewy tip of her tongue.

Cain went rigid. Every hard muscle in his body grew taught, and reaction rippled over him as if his world had exploded with the violence of his response. Yet he didn't move to gather her more fully into his arms. Nor did he kiss her with the passion she knew was simmering just below the surface.

Dazed with these strange, unrelenting waves of longing, Leah kissed him with a lifetime of suppressed womanhood stored in her heart.

His mouth played over hers, tasting and nibbling, taking and giving. Giving so much that Leah's world spiraled crazily.

Her arms moved possessively over the hard-muscled grace of his back, glorying as his bronze muscles rippled under her fingers. Pressed together as they were, Cain pushed the covers down from her waist so that his hard thighs molded her against him.

After what seemed like forever, he lifted his mouth from hers and took in deep, shuddering breaths as he cradled her face between his hands. Leah covered his hands with her own, turning her head so that she could kiss the inside of his palm. Cain's reaction was immediate as he slowly, languorously buried his mouth in hers until a need, a desire she had never known, sent flames shooting through her. Straining to be closer to him, her hips rocked, seeking more.

His hand cupped her breast, and Leah thought she would die with the exquisite sensations that raced through her. His thumb made circling caresses over her pebble-hard nipples until she moaned. But when his hand lowered to her flat stomach, it was Cain who groaned. The sound throbbed in Leah's ears, and she tightened her grip on him, teasing him with her tongue, giving him biting little kisses over his face and ears until his mouth branded hers in burning, searing possession.

Without warning, Cain tore his mouth from hers and raised himself. He took in deep, measured breaths as if he were holding on to the last vestige of his control.

"Cain," she whispered, not knowing what had stopped him.

"Leah," he murmured, and gathered her in his arms. "Dear, sweet Leah, shall I go on?"

The air felt trapped in her lungs.

"You know what I want?" he asked slowly.

"Yes." Her whispered voice trembled. "Oh, yes. I want you."

He hesitated for only a moment. His hand reached for her neck, locating the delicate chain that held the gold heart. With a vicious jerk, he broke the chain and tossed it aside. The sound of it hitting the wall barely registered in Leah's passion.

When dawn came to lighten the room, Leah gave a soft sigh of satisfaction. Cain was cuddling her, his hand cupping her breast. He had made love to her last night until she thought she would die from the pure joy of it.

"Morning," he whispered near her ear.

"Morning." Maybe she should feel shy and awkward, but she didn't. Rolling onto her back, she looped her arms around his neck. "I had the most wonderful dream last night."

He nuzzled her throat, fiercely holding her to him. "That wasn't a dream."

"It had to have been," she teased lovingly. "Nothing in my life has ever been that good."

"Maybe we should have a repeat performance so you'll know," he said, his voice hoarse with tenderness.

"I think we should," she breathed. "Oh, Cain, I think we should."

The island became their personal paradise. With less than a week left of the expedition, they spent long hours with each other, never speaking of the morrow or life back in San Diego. At night, Cain would reach for her, loving her with a tenderness that managed to steal her breath.

During the day he was often at her side, taking her picture. Leah was uncomfortable with that, but didn't want anything to ruin this idyllic happiness.

With a deep sense of regret, Leah packed for their return trip to San Diego. They had found this complete sharing of themselves so late, Leah feared it would all be ruined once they returned to civilization.

On their last morning together, Leah lay in Cain's arms, dreading the time Hugh would arrive. Their luggage was packed, their gear lined up in the outer room ready to be delivered to the boat.

Almost shyly, Leah dressed, pulling the jeans over her slim, narrow hips. Not until she was finished did she realize that Cain had been watching her. There seemed little need for modesty now, and yet she blushed when she discovered he'd been studying her so intently.

"Hugh will be here any time now," she murmured, glancing away.

"Yes," Cain answered awkwardly.

She was headed for the door when Cain stopped her. "Leah."

She turned, uncertain.

"I thought you might want this." The gold necklace Siggy had given her was dangling from his hand.

Leah couldn't have been more shocked if he'd slapped her face. She stared at it, and the color drained from her motionless features.

Then she understood as clearly as if he were shouting it at her. Their time together was over. When they arrived back in San Diego, he would go about his life, and she should do the same.

Her chin trembled, and she bit into her bottom lip as she reached across the short distance and snapped the gold heart from his grasp.

Chapter Eight

Leah!" Surprise and delight lit up the aged face as Dr. Brewster stood and moved to the front of his desk. "My dear, you look absolutely radiant." He gave her a brief hug and, shaking his round face with wonder, took a step back. "How tan you are. You remind me more of a golden goddess than a capable scientist."

Leah's thick lashes lowered with the praise, not knowing how to deal with such wholehearted approval. "Thank you."

"Where's Cain?"

Leah's heart constricted painfully. She didn't know where he was. Not exactly. Somewhere in San Diego, she assumed. He'd dropped her off at her apartment, his face a tight mask, wiped clean of expression. His last words were that he'd contact her when the film had been developed. With her heart crying out to stop him, Leah had given a perfunctory nod and told him that would be fine. Neither one mentioned the divorce, although according to their written agreement it was to take place within a week of their return.

"Leah?" Dr. Brewster prompted. "I was asking you about Cain."

"He'll be contacting you soon." Her answering smile was weak and a little wobbly. Being without Cain was still so new. She had tried to sound reassuring and happy but knew that she had failed miserably.

"Sit down," he ordered, his voice laced with concern. "You look like you're dead on your feet. I'm so anxious to hear of your findings. Tell me everything."

Leah did as he bid, sitting on the chair opposite her mentor's huge desk. She didn't know where to begin. "Cain was a wonderful help," she murmured, lacing her fingers together tightly in her lap. "He helped me in every aspect of the expedition and still managed to obtain some fantastic photographs."

"I knew he would." Walking to the other side of the small office, Dr. Brewster poured Leah a cup of tea, adding two lumps of sugar to the steaming liquid.

Dr. Brewster was well aware that Leah drank her tea straight, and the action brought a sad smile to her face. Like Cain, Dr. Brewster seemed intent on fattening her up.

"I personally chose Cain Hawkins," he explained, and handed Leah the cup and saucer. "Of all the people I know in this world, Cain seemed the best man for the job."

"Yes, of course." Leah's gaze refused to meet his.

"I can't tell you how pleased I am that you two resolved your differences."

A bubble of laughter nearly escaped from her throat. She wondered what Dr. Brewster would think if he knew to what extent they had settled their "differences."

Facing such eager enthusiasm, Leah began to tell him about her adventures on the island. They talked nonstop for an hour, until Dr. Brewster was reluctantly forced to leave for class. He hugged her again as she rose, a gesture Leah found strangely comforting.

"I'll be bringing the documents in to you at the end of the week," she assured him as they stepped out of his office. Together they headed across the lush rolling hills of lawn that comprised the university campus.

Two young men dressed in tattered cutoffs, probably freshmen, were throwing a Frisbee. With a gentle smile, Leah watched the red disk float through space. Once she would have found this sight disconcerting. The university was an institution of higher learning, not a playground.

When Leah returned her attention to Dr. Brewster, his brow was knit in thick lines of concentration. "Bring Cain with you the next time you come."

Leah dropped her gaze and nodded miserably. "I'll do that."

Back at her apartment, Leah examined the luxury that surrounded her. She would gladly have traded it all for another day with Cain in the stark island hut that had been their home. She hadn't thought she'd miss him so terribly, but this ache was far worse than anything she'd ever known. The pain in her heart was a thousand times heavier than any hurt she'd ever suffered.

They'd only been back three days, and it felt more like three years. The nights were the worst. A hundred times she'd rolled over, unconsciously searching for the warm, loving body beside her. Her thoughts were shameless. It wasn't only his warmth she missed, but his touch, slow and infinitely gentle. His lovemaking had never been hurried or urgent. He'd loved her as if they'd had all the time in the world.

Without thinking, she moved her fingers to her throat as she recalled in vivid detail the way Cain would slide his hand over her throat and down over her breasts, circling her nipples until they rose proudly. Leah had shivered with delight, teasing him with her own fingers. She had thrilled with unexpected pleasure at how responsive his body was to the mere brush of her fingertips as they lightly grazed his chest. In the darkened room, Leah could refuse him nothing, completely entrusting herself into his gentle, skilled hands. He'd whispered the most wonderful things to her, his voice hoarse and tender, and not once had she doubted him. For those few, all-too-short days, the world had been theirs. Little had she realized their utopian happiness was to be so short-lived. From the moment Hugh arrived to deliver them to Ruaehu, Cain had been like a polite stranger.

Leah drew in a long steady breath as her gaze fixed on the telephone. He'd promised to call; with everything that was in her, Leah demanded that the phone ring. She was dying to hear from him, though she had no idea what she'd say once he did. Nonetheless, her whole concentration was focused on the telephone that stood tauntingly silent.

When the doorbell rang later that afternoon, Leah's heart raced until she was forced to stretch out a hand and grip the kitchen counter to steady herself. If it was Cain, she was determined to meet his gaze with the same lack of emotion that he had shown toward her. With her head held high, she would greet him coolly and invite him inside. Then, with complete indifference, she would ask him to sit down. She was determined to do nothing to ease his discomfort when he told her that the past three days had taught him he couldn't live without her. Only when he'd revealed the depth of his love and humbly come to her would she disclose that she, too, had come to love him. Against her will, of course.

The doorbell chimed impatiently a second time before Leah moved. She forced a plastic smile on her tight lips and opened the door.

The disappointment that surged through her was so strong that she was forced to swallow back a cry. Siggy, dressed impeccably in a pale-blue leisure suit and navy-blue bow tie, stood on the opposite side of the threshold.

"Leah...darling." He took her by the shoulders and kissed her lightly on the forehead. "My heavens, what have you done to yourself?"

"Hello, Siggy." The happiness she should have felt at seeing her fiancé simply wasn't there. Only an aching heart for the man she loved, the man who hadn't come. Cain.

Siggy slid an arm around her narrow waist and impetuously closed the door with his foot. Thinking himself devilishly suave, he chuckled and swung her around to embrace her tightly. Leah gave him all the response of a rag doll. She purposely hadn't contacted Siggy. She didn't want him to know she was in town until she knew what was going to happen between her and Cain.

"Let me look at you," Siggy said, stepping back and frowning. "Your hair," he moaned, shaking his head. "Is that hippie photographer responsible for destroying your lovely golden tresses?" His mouth tightened, and with a display of anger he smashed his clenched fist into the open palm of his other hand. "That Hawkins man did this to you, didn't he? Now don't bother to defend him, Leah. It's just the kind of stupid stunt I'd expect of someone like Hawkins."

She managed to contain the laughter that welled in her throat. "I'm the one responsible," she explained.

"One can only wonder what else he forced you to submit to."

"Siggy," Leah groaned with a decided lack of patience. "Cain didn't force me to submit to anything."

Stroking his chin, Siggy nodded thoughtfully. "That's what he said."

"*He* said?" Desperately, Leah's gaze cornered Siggy's. "He's talked to you?" Her mind whirled in fury. Cain had no right to contact Siggy. God only knew what he'd said to him.

With a snort, Siggy crossed the room, sat on the leather sofa and crossed his legs. Leah sat across from him, studying his tight features.

"Threatened me is more like it," Siggy continued indignantly. "He said if I didn't make you happy then I'd be answering to him personally." A finger edged the shirt collar from his neck as he cleared his throat. "I do care for you, Leah." As he spoke, a flushed color crept up from his neck. "Deeply. Enough to remember that your hair will grow back and that eventually... you'll be my same lovely Leah once again."

"Oh, Siggy." How could she explain that she would never be the same again? Never wanted to be. Now that she was back from Kahu, she realized that what she'd shared with him was only a pale imitation of what love was supposed to be between a man and a woman.

"Yes... darling?" He leaned forward, bracing his elbows on his knees as he looked adoringly into Leah's deep, hazel eyes.

Straightening, Leah offered him a tight smile. "I... I think that I should be completely honest with you."

"Yes?" He stiffened, his action mirroring Leah's.

"While we... Cain and I... were on the island..." Leah paused and sucked in a troubled breath. This was a thousand times more difficult that she'd ever dreamed. She didn't feel ashamed over what had happened. Never ashamed.

"What are you trying to say?" Siggy prompted, moving closer to the edge of the cushion.

"There was only one bed on the island."

"And so you slept together?" His words were low and shocked.

"We had to," she returned forcefully. "There was only the one bed."

"And..." Siggy paused and cleared his throat. "And did you do...anything else?"

Closing her eyes, Leah nodded.

"I...see," Siggy said with infinite sadness as he pushed himself upright. "I guess it's only to be expected. The two of you alone on the island like that." The hurt-little-boy look was back again. Squaring his shoulders, Siggy met her gaze. "I think you should know that I forgive you, Leah."

It was on the tip of her tongue to scream at him that she didn't want his forgiveness. She had no regrets. Instead, she nodded and smiled, knowing what it must have cost him to say that. "Thank you," she murmured gently.

He wiped a hand across his face and dramatically pinched the bridge of his nose. "I need time to think."

"Of course you do."

"I love you, don't misunderstand me, but in the light of what happened between you and this Hawkins fellow, maybe we shouldn't see each other for a few days. We both need time to think things through."

"I understand." She stood and clasped her hands in front of her.

"There isn't a possibility...?" he mumbled, and gave a small cough. "You wouldn't be pregnant, would you?"

Pregnant? The word hit Leah's mind with the impact of a hand grenade. Of course there was that possibility, but crazily it hadn't occurred to her.

"Leah?"

"I don't know," she answered honestly.

"I see." Siggy edged his way toward the front door. "Let's say the first of next week?"

Leah looked at him blankly. "Pardon?"

"I'll call you the first of the week. We can have dinner."

The offer flabbergasted her even more than the possibility she could be bearing the fruit of those last days on the island with Cain. "Fine."

"I'll call you." His hand was on the doorknob. "I do care for you, Leah."

"Thank you, Siggy."

The door closed after him, and Leah leaned against it and placed a hand on her flat abdomen. A smile touched her features and grew and grew until she was on the verge of breaking into great, gulping laughter. A baby. Emotion welled in her heart as she raised her head, lifting her eyes to the heavens, and offered a silent prayer.

Heaven answered her three days later. A visit to a local gynecologist confirmed that she was indeed in the early stages of pregnancy. Happiness flowed through her until she wanted to dance and sing and laugh. Maybe she should be experiencing bitter regrets. Instead she felt like stopping strangers on the street to announce her wonderful news.

The gold band around her finger that had once felt awkward and heavy now seemed right, almost a part of her. Once home, she opened the refrigerator and poured herself a glass of milk. With a baby to consider she wouldn't be skipping any more meals. Cain had finally gotten his wish and was responsible for fattening her up. The thought produced a happy laugh.

Cain. She'd have to tell him. That was when the niggling apprehensions started to mount. How would her news alter their relationship? Would Cain insist on delaying the divorce? With his life-style, Leah was confident he wouldn't try to take the baby from her. A child would only complicate his life, and he wouldn't want complications. That was fine, because she wanted this baby very much.

Ironically, the first person she thought to call was Siggy. Her heart was burning to contact her mother, but her family didn't even know she was married. There would be plenty of time later to talk to her mother. In fact, she would probably have to move back to the farm later in the pregnancy. She'd want to be with people who loved her.

Her finger shook as she punched out Siggy's office number.

The line rang three times, and when he answered Siggy sounded slightly flustered. "Harcharik here."

"Siggy, it's Leah."

"Leah." His voice filled with pleasure and surprise. "How are you?"

"Wonderful." Curtailing her happiness was impossible; even with Siggy. "I went to the doctor today."

A stark silence followed her announcement. "And?"

"And I'm going to be a mother."

Another shocked silence followed. "I see."

"Listen, Siggy," Leah murmured gravely. "I can understand if you decide you don't ever want to see me again. I realize that this is a shock to you."

"How are you feeling?" he interrupted her sharply. "You aren't ill or anything?"

"No, no, I've never felt better." Her spirits were soaring to the highest heavens because her love for Cain was bearing a precious fruit. How could she have believed for even a moment that what they shared wouldn't produce a child? It had been so beautiful, so right.

"You sound happy about it," he whispered accusingly.

"Oh, I am. Very, very happy."

"I see."

Leah wondered if he really understood any of this. "I apologize for hurting you, Siggy," she whispered contritely. "That was never my intention."

"Yes, well, the best intentions aren't going to change the facts, are they?"

"Not in this case."

"Goodbye, Leah," he said, his soft voice cracking, and almost immediately the line was disconnected.

For the first time since hearing the test results, Leah experienced regret. She hadn't meant to hurt Siggy, but clearly she had.

Replacing the telephone receiver, Leah curled up on the couch and reached for a book the doctor had given her. She read it straight through, so engrossed that Siggy was soon driven from her mind.

When the doorbell chimed, Leah glanced up with surprise. If it was Cain, she wouldn't know how to tell him about the baby. Maybe it would be best not to say anything.

But when she opened the door, it wasn't Cain who stared back at her. Siggy, white-faced and obviously flustered, met her gaze.

"I've been thinking," he said as he strolled into the room. "The baby doesn't matter."

"What?" Leah looked at him with openmouthed disbelief.

"You heard me. We can raise it as our own."

Her jaw remained open and refused to close.

"Of course, we couldn't tell Mother that the baby isn't mine. That would shock her into an early grave."

"Siggy." His name was all she could manage.

"I love you, Leah. I've always wanted you to be my wife. I refuse to allow this unfortunate experience with Hawkins to ruin our lives."

Chapter Nine

Cain phoned Leah the first part of the next week. She'd been awaiting his call for so long, but she made herself answer calmly.

"Hello, Leah."

"Cain." Her hand tightened around the receiver as she forced her voice to remain level and devoid of emotion. He sounded tired, and his voice dipped with a trace of impatience.

"How have you been?"

Miserable. Lonely. Afraid. Excited. "Fine," she murmured finally.

"Would it be inconvenient for me to stop by for a few minutes?" he inquired with starched politeness.

How could they talk to each other like this? Leah's heart cried. It was as if he had never held her in his arms or whispered that he ached all the way to his bones with wanting her. Apparently, he'd blocked out the love they'd shared on Kahu as effectively as if he were changing rolls of film in his camera. Leah wanted to cry out at the injustice of it. Instead, she found her voice and assured him he was welcome anytime.

"I'll be there in fifteen minutes."

"Good," she said, her voice as flat as his had been.

Pacing the living room carpet, Leah tried desperately to decide what she should tell him. She found the irony of the situation highly amusing. She had been the least attractive girl in her high school. The brain. The girl most likely to succeed outside the bedroom. And here she was pregnant by one man, with another eagerly waiting for her to divorce Cain so they could be married. Leah didn't doubt Siggy's sincerity. He would be a good father to her child. And he certainly must love her to be willing to accept these unusual circumstances.

With the minutes ticking away, Leah made her decision. If Cain sauntered in and asked that they make the arrangements for the divorce, then she wouldn't let him know she was going to have a baby. It was important that they not stay married simply because of the new life they had created. She didn't want to trap him.

On the other hand, if he came and told her he was miserable and had missed her dreadfully, that would change everything. Then Leah would tell him she was pregnant. From there a reconciliation would come naturally. Leah yearned with all her heart to tell Cain how much she loved him, but after the way he'd so heartlessly handed her Siggy's necklace, pride wouldn't allow her to speak first.

The doorbell chimed, and inhaling a steadying breath, Leah strode across the apartment and opened the door.

"Hello, Cain," she greeted, even before looking to see who it was.

"Leah." He marched into the apartment, carrying a briefcase. His hair was mussed as if he'd raked his hand through it several times. Finely etched lines fanned out from his eyes, giving the impression he hadn't slept well in several nights. Yet when her gaze met his, she saw the sparks of anger igniting. He looked as if he couldn't decide whether to haul her into his arms and kiss her senseless or push her over his knee and spank her unmercifully.

She smiled uncertainly, hesitated, then gestured toward the sofa. "Would you care to sit down? I've got a beer, if you want one."

His hot gaze shot to her. "When in hell did you start drinking beer?"

"I . . . I didn't."

"You bought it for me?"

Damn. It had been an insane thing to do. From the morning Cain had dropped her off at the apartment, Leah had known he was coming back. Ever since that day, she'd been doing little things to prepare for their meeting. Buying a six-pack of his favorite beer had seemed the natural thing to do.

"Yes, I picked up a six-pack at the store this week," she answered thoughtfully, lowering her gaze so he couldn't read her eyes.

"Why?"

Because I've thought of you every minute since we left the island. Because doing a wifely thing like buying you beer made the ache inside me lessen just a little. Because your child is growing in my womb and I'm so happy I want to shout it from the hilltops. "I . . . I knew you'd probably want one," she supplied lamely, still centering her gaze on the carpet. "Do you want one or not?" she asked with a trace of defiance, more angry with herself for buying it than with him for making an issue of it.

"Have you got anything stronger?"

"No."

"Then a beer is fine."

At least getting it for him gave her a few moments to compose herself. Cain was sitting on the edge of the sofa when she reappeared, his face hard and unreadable. He accepted the open bottle mechanically and, without looking, set it aside.

Stiffly, Leah sat opposite him, waiting.

Slowly, gently, his gaze moved over her, and in his eyes Leah witnessed uncertainty, indecision and a multitude of doubts. She longed to reach out and reassure him, but they both remained as they were—silent, intimate strangers. A lump of desolation swelled in her throat, and Leah swallowed back the tears that threatened to spill at the least provocation.

She spoke first, needing to break the horrible silence. "Have you developed the film?"

Cain shook himself lightly and nodded. "Some of my best work is in those photographs."

"I knew it would be," she said.

He set the briefcase on the coffee table and pushed back the lock. The clicking sound vibrated across the room. Without a word, he removed the first one and handed it to her. It was one of her, taken when she hadn't expected it that night in Perth when they were meeting Hugh for dinner. Leah recalled how upset she'd been at the time and how she had attempted to look away. It was that night that they'd walked on the beach and Cain had kissed her for the first time.

"Well?"

Speechless, Leah stared at it and shook her head. He'd caught her with the element of surprise lighting up her face. Her eyes glowed, and a soft smile turned up the edges of her mouth appealingly. "It's very nice." Probably the most flattering photo ever taken of her.

"Now look at this." He handed her the second photo.

This time Leah gave a small gasp of surprise. This one had been taken while she was sitting at the cliff's edge. She was wearing white shorts and a red pin-striped cotton top that accentuated her deep tan. Her hair had been cut, the short style wind-tossed and ruffled about her face. She was laughing into the lens, waving her hand, yelling at Cain to take his camera away. She didn't want her picture taken. Again, Leah was shocked at how attractive the photo made her look. Cain had captured her image in such a way that she looked stunningly attractive. No, beautiful.

Speechless, Leah stared at him, shaking her head. Numbly, she accepted the third and last photo from his outstretched hand. This one had been taken the day before they left. She was walking along the beach, her arms reaching to him, imploring Cain to put the camera down and come to her so she could kiss him. Her eyes were sparkling with warmth and laughter and so full of love that she wondered how Cain could ever look at it and not realize her feelings for him.

"Well," Cain demanded harshly. "Do you see it?"

Leah set the photo aside. Unwanted, embarrassing tears dammed her eyes, threatening to spill. "How'd you make me so beautiful?" she whispered.

Cain cocked his head and gave her a fiery glare. "Are you fishing for compliments?"

Leah stood and walked to the other end of the room; her arms hugged her waist. "Of course not," she answered softly. "But in each one of those pictures, you made me something I will never be."

Cain rose to his feet and tiredly wiped his eyes. "What do you mean?"

"My eyes." She walked back to the coffee table and picked up the first picture. "Look. You made my murky brown-green eyes look radiant."

"Murky eyes?" Cain repeated, and slowly shook his head. "They've never been that. You have an unusual eye color that reminds me of aged brandy."

"Me?" Leah flattened her hand across her breast.

"Damn it, Leah, I didn't bring these photos to discuss the color of your eyes."

"But . . . but you made me look so pretty," she argued. "How did you do it?"

Cain jerked his hands inside his pants pockets, then angrily pulled them out again as if he weren't sure if he could refrain from shaking her. "Do you or do you not see anything different in these photos?"

So he was back to that again. "Yes," she barked, "you made me . . . pretty."

"And that's all you see?"

"Yes." What else could he possibly mean? Magnetically Leah's gaze was drawn back to the three pictures. Once, a long time ago, Cain had told her that he took pictures exactly the way he viewed the subject. She couldn't keep her gaze from the three images. Cain saw her like this? Beautiful, warm, full of life? Her heart swelled with appreciation. No one had ever thought she was beautiful. Not even Siggy. But if Cain could see all the love in her eyes that shone only for him, then why had he given her back Siggy's necklace?

"Leah." Cain murmured her name, pacing the floor. "Look at me." He stopped and turned to her, his face twisted with anguish and some unspeakable torment. "Are you pregnant?"

Automatically her hand flew to her flat stomach. Cain knew, but how?

"Are you?" he demanded with a wealth of emotion, his fists clenched at his side.

Words refused to come. Nodding seemed a monumental feat.

"You've seen a doctor?"

Again all she could do was answer him with a brief nod of her head. "How did you know?"

A crooked smile slashed across his face. "The picture," he said cryptically. "It's in your eyes in the last photo, the one taken on the beach."

Sinking into the chair, Leah picked up the one he'd mentioned and studied it again. Heavens, she'd only been a few days along. As far as she could see there wasn't anything different about that picture.

Silence reigned in the confined quarters as Cain continued pacing. He stopped and regarded her with narrow eyes. "Are you going to marry lover boy?" Cain demanded next, revealing none of his thoughts.

"I . . . I don't know yet," she answered honestly.

"Does he know you're pregnant?"

"Yes."

Cain looked furious enough to shake her senseless. "You told him, but not me."

"I was going to let you know."

"When? After the baby was born?"

"No," she answered weakly. "I've been waiting for you to get in touch with me."

"Don't give me that," he tore out angrily. "You could have found me if you really wanted to tell me the news. Were you waiting until after we were divorced and you were married to Sidney? Which brings me to another point." He paused and leaned forward, his hands gripping the back of the sofa. "Is that spineless idiot prepared to marry you while you're carrying my child?"

"Don't call Siggy that," she protested.

"Just answer the question," he barked.

"Yes...Siggy said it didn't matter to him. He wants children. He'll be a good father."

"And I won't?"

Leah didn't know it was possible for anyone to look so angry. "I didn't mean to imply that."

"Then just exactly what did you mean to imply?" His question held blazing animosity.

Leah dropped her gaze, suddenly feeling weak and a little shaky. "Nothing," she mumbled, her weakness reflected in her voice.

Instantly, Cain was kneeling at her side, his look contrite. "Are you feeling sick?"

"Just a little," she murmured, fighting to keep her voice level. All this anger and bitterness was taking its toll. "I'm sorry," she gulped miserably, "I didn't mean for any of this to happen. The consequences never occurred to me. I suppose it was stupid of me."

His eyes cut into hers as if he were penetrating her soul. "Are you sorry?"

"No." She wanted to tell him so much more but found she couldn't. If he couldn't tell that she loved him by looking at those pictures, then explaining the joy she felt at discovering she was pregnant wouldn't help.

"You're going to keep the baby?"

Her eyes flew to him in horror. How could he imagine anything else? "Of course."

"And you and...Sidney are going to go ahead with your wedding plans?"

"I told you I don't know yet," she cried.

"When will you know?"

Forcing herself to her feet, Leah lifted one shoulder in a shrug. "In a few days, I imagine." She longed to scream at Cain that everything depended on him. But it wouldn't do any good.

"You'll let me know right away?"

"Yes, yes, of course." The muscles of her throat were constricting painfully, and Leah knew she was just seconds away from bursting into tears. As it was, her legs felt like rubber and her heart was pounding so loud it was a miracle Cain didn't hear it. Sick with defeat and failure, she walked to the door and held it open for him. "I'll call you by the end of the week."

Carelessly, Cain stuffed the photos inside the briefcase. Leah knew by the furious way he was handling the pictures that he wished his hands were around her neck. Straightening, he stalked to the front door. "I'll be waiting."

The apartment was as silent as death after Cain left. Feeling exhausted, Leah lay down and was shocked to wake up two and a half hours later. She felt she could sleep her life away. Whether that was because of the baby or a desire to escape the dilemma that faced her, Leah didn't know.

At dinnertime her appetite was nonexistent, but she forced down scrambled eggs, toast and a tall glass of milk. Cain would be pleased to know she was at least eating properly.

After her extended afternoon nap, Leah had trouble sleeping that night. With her hands tucked under her head, she stared at the ceiling of the darkened room. Her mind whirled with ideas. The spare room she now used as her office could easily be transformed into a nursery. And although her skill was limited, she was capable of sewing what clothes the baby would need. As for the blankets and such, she'd always wanted to know how to knit. There was no better time to learn than the present.

Someone pounding against the front door startled her, and she bolted upright. Had she imagined the commotion? A repeat of the pounding assured her she hadn't. Dragging the robe from the bottom of the bed with her, Leah turned on the hallway light and moved into the living room.

"Who is it?" she called without opening the door.

"Cain," he answered, and continued beating on the door. "Let me in. I want to talk to you. I demand to talk to you." His voice was slurred and angry.

Concerned more that he'd do himself harm than with any fear for herself, Leah unlatched the lock and opened the front door.

Cain staggered into the room and made a three-hundred-sixty-degree turn attempting to find her. With his index finger pointing to the ceiling, he laughed loudly. "There you are."

"You're drunk," she announced accusingly, smelling the offensive odor of whiskey. In all the time they'd worked together, Leah had never known Cain to overindulge. Not in alcohol.

"So you noticed."

"For heaven's sake, sit down before you hurt yourself." Convinced he'd never make it to the sofa without help, Leah slipped an arm around his muscular waist.

As if he found her touch painful, Cain froze and gave a small cry. He pulled her into his arms, crushing her against his chest until Leah was unable to move. He buried his face in the silken curve of her neck and breathed in a deep, shuddering sigh. "Oh, Leah, my sweet Leah," he muttered unevenly; then, stiffening, he pushed her away. "Before you tell me your decision, I want you to know I've made one of my own."

Leah's blood was pounding in her ears. "Yes?" she murmured meekly. Even if he admitted that he loved her in a drunken stupor, it wouldn't matter.

"You can have your stupid divorce," he shouted with a harsh edge, cutting through her meager defenses. "But you aren't marrying your Sidney creep while you're carrying my child. Understand?"

Tears stung the back of her eyes, and Leah boldly met his fierce gaze. She held herself stiff, her whole body tensing into a rigid line. So he was going to give her a divorce. What difference did it make if it was before or after the baby arrived?

"I see," she said quietly.

"I don't want that stuffed shirt raising my kid," he declared, collapsing onto the sofa as if his legs would no longer support him.

So that was his reasoning. Not that he loved her. Not that he cared about the baby. Not that he couldn't bear to live his life without her. No, he didn't want Siggy raising his son. "You're drunk," she said, her eyes limpid pools of misery.

"That I am. Does it please you to know you have the power to drive me to the bottle?"

Hands on her hips, Leah glared down at him and shook her head. "At this moment," she confessed, "it thrills me."

Suddenly she stormed into the other room, then returned with a blanket and pillow. "Look, right now I don't want to hear a thing from you. But I can't let you drive home like this. You're staying here."

"Good," he said, groping for the sofa arm to help him stand upright. His face fell when he saw the blanket and pillow in her arms. "You don't honestly expect me to sleep in here? This sofa is as hard as a rock. I'll toss and turn the entire night." His gaze slid longingly down the hall to her bedroom.

"Good. A miserable night on a hard, cold surface is exactly what you need to sober you up." She tossed the pillow at his face, then whirled around. "And don't you think of leaving. The minute you walk out that door, I'm phoning the police. You have no business endangering your life or anyone else's by driving."

"Yes, Your Honor." He saluted her mockingly. The action caused him to lose his balance, and he teetered awkwardly before falling onto the sofa, his head hitting the arm. He let out a muffled curse.

A smile curved Leah's soft mouth as she left him alone, Cain rubbing the side of his head.

The smell of fresh coffee woke her the following morning. After donning her clothes as quickly as possible, Leah hurried into the kitchen. Cain was sitting at the table, his head cushioned between his palms, his elbows propped on the tabletop.

"Morning."

His response was little more than a grumble.

Leah took a mug down from the cupboard and poured herself some coffee. The aspirin was tucked in the back of a drawer; she slid it out and set the plastic bottle in front of Cain. The slight sound made him grimace.

Without speaking, he flipped off the lid and shook two tablets into the palm of his hand, then downed them without water.

"Thanks," he mumbled, still not glancing her way.

"You're welcome."

"Do you have to sound so damn cheerful?" Again he scowled at the pain his own voice caused him.

"No." Carefully she slid out the chair and sat across from him.

"Good. Now..." He paused and sucked in a breath. "Quietly, please, tell me what I said last night."

Her palms cupped the mug, seeking its warmth. "Not much." Her voice was barely above a whisper. "You said you'd give me the divorce after the baby was born."

He lowered his hands for the first time. "Well?" His gaze sought hers. "Do you agree?"

"No." She gave an uncompromising shake of her head. What difference did it make when they were divorced? The only thing Cain wanted to do was ruin any chance of happiness she'd have with Siggy.

"Why not?" he barked, and widened his eyes at the pain that shot through his head.

"Because our agreement states that you're to give me the divorce one week after our departure from Kahu. That time limit is long past."

"That was before—"

"We didn't list any extenuating circumstances that would prolong our affiliation."

"You call our marriage an affiliation?" Cain emitted a harsh laugh.

"Why?" Leah ventured timidly.

"Why what?"

"Why do you want to wait . . . you know . . . for the divorce?"

His mouth went rigid. "I told you I didn't want that pompous stuffed shirt delivering my kid."

What he'd said was that he didn't want Siggy *raising* their child. Cain didn't expect her to notice the difference, but she had.

Lowering her gaze, Leah traced her finger in lazy circles around the rim of the coffee mug. "Is...is that the only reason?"

"Should there be another one?" he challenged.

"No," she whispered soberly. "No reason that I know."

"And?"

"And I say no. The divorce will proceed according to the agreement."

Abruptly he stood up, knocking the kitchen chair to the floor with a horrible crash. "Fine. Have it your way. Can you be ready by ten tomorrow morning?"

"Ready?" So soon? her heart cried in anguish.

"Yes, we'll fly to Reno and be done with it. You can have your freedom and your precious Sidney."

It took a full minute for her to compose herself enough to raise her head and meet his rigid gaze. "I'll be ready."

Chapter Ten

The front door clicked shut behind Cain. Slowly, with excruciating effort, Leah lowered her lashes to accept the pain that seared all the way through her soul. She'd gambled and lost. Cain would grant her the divorce and be done with her.

Her fingers tightened around the ceramic handle of the mug, and she forced down her first sip. The hot coffee burned her throat, but Leah welcomed the pain. She marveled at her composure. How could she sit and drink coffee when her whole world had just shattered into a thousand pieces? Tears burned for release, and her throat grew thick with the effort to suppress their flow.

Her gaze dropped to her hand and the gold band that adorned her ring finger. This plain gold band had been Cain's mother's, and she had given it up freely. Tomorrow Leah would be forced to relinquish it, too. But Leah knew she would face a lifetime of doubts without this gold ring. It seemed so much a part of her now that she couldn't imagine life without it.

Her melancholy persisted for the remainder of the day. Siggy arrived for their dinner date at precisely six o'clock and studied her covertly as she opened the door.

Leah let him in and nervously clasped her hands in front of her. She didn't feel up to an evening in Siggy's favorite restaurant, watching him down another plate of zucchini quiche.

Briefly, he placed his hands on her shoulders and kissed her cheek. Not for the first time, Leah noted that he treated her as if he were an affectionate older brother rather than a fiancé.

"Sit down." She motioned toward the sofa. For a half second she toyed with telling Siggy that Cain had spent the night. She couldn't; it would be too cruel. But something in her wanted to know if he'd forgive her for that, too. Somehow she suspected he would.

"How are you feeling...darling?" The endearment almost stuck on his tongue, and Leah hid a sad smile. Siggy didn't love her any more than Cain did. She was the prize in a battle of fierce male pride. Cain couldn't tolerate the bespectacled, nonathletic Siggy, and Siggy was determined to prove that what he lacked in the he-man department he could overcome with brains and persistence. He was the preferable of the two, and Leah would prove it to the egotistical Cain

Hawkins. Though by this time, she was thoroughly disgusted with them both.

Sinking into the deep, cushioned chair opposite Siggy, Leah guiltily lowered her gaze. "I'm not feeling all that well tonight," she murmured tightly. The ache in her heart had made this the worst day of her life. Putting on a cheerful facade for Siggy tonight was beyond her.

"I can order something and bring it back here," Siggy offered eagerly.

Even that was more than she could bear. All she wanted was a few hours alone to prepare herself for the ordeal in the morning.

"Cain and I are flying to Reno tomorrow," she supplied reluctantly.

Siggy slid closer to the edge of the leather sofa. "For the divorce?"

Her fingernails cut unmercifully into her palms as she nodded her head.

"But, darling, that's wonderful. Now you'll be free for us to marry." He sounded so eager, so pleased. "I'll make you a good husband, Leah," he said almost reverently. "Making you my wife will be one of my life's greatest accomplishments."

"Siggy..." Leah swallowed, profoundly touched that this man was willing to overlook so much to marry her, no matter what his reasons.

"Yes?" He gave her a nervous glance.

"I can't marry you."

"Leah." His hurt response was immediate. "But you must for... for the baby's sake. I've already explained that as long as Mother doesn't know, I'm perfectly happy to be its surrogate father."

Standing, Leah walked around the coffee table and sat beside a flustered and unhappy Siggy. Taking his hand in her own, Leah offered him a genuine smile and tentatively touched the side of his face, wanting to ease some of the hurt and disappointment.

Siggy's cheeks flowered with color. Clearing his throat, he pushed up his glasses from the bridge of his nose. "I'm hoping you'll reconsider, Leah."

"I want you to know I'll always treasure you as one of my closest and dearest friends."

"But... but I want to be so much more," he entreated on a faint pleading note.

"Don't you understand that I'm a married woman? I'm going to have a child by my husband."

"But... but you said it wasn't a real marriage. You said that you and this Hawkins fellow were getting a divorce in the morning. You said that everything was going to work out fine and that nothing was going to happen between you on the island."

"But it did," she countered softly. "I'll have my baby by myself, and someday, God willing, Cain and I will be together again. I love him, Siggy." It was the first time Leah had openly admitted her feelings. Ironically, it was Siggy who heard her admission, and not Cain.

For a full minute Siggy didn't speak. Hoping to reassure him, Leah squeezed his hand. She was convinced he was about to burst into tears, and she couldn't bear that.

"Nothing I can say will change your mind, will it?" he asked again stiffly, and tugged his hand free from her light grasp.

"I'm afraid not," she answered honestly.

"Just as I thought." Proudly he rose to his feet, holding his back rigid. His mouth was compressed so tight that his lips were an unnatural shade of white. "In that case, I must ask for the necklace I gave you. I can't see wasting good money on a...on a vixen like you."

Leah managed to restrain a hurt gasp. She forgave Siggy without his ever asking her pardon. He was hurt and angry, and in his pain he was lashing back at her. Leah understood and granted him that much pride.

She did as he asked, retreating into her bedroom and returning a few moments later with the necklace.

Siggy gave her a long, penetrating look, and his mouth twisted with open disdain.

Awash with regrets, Leah held her trembling chin high and watched him go. No matter why they'd parted, or Siggy's feelings toward her, Leah would always have a special place in her heart for him. Before Cain arrived in her life, Siggy had been the only man to care about her, genuinely care.

The next morning Leah packed an overnight case. Cain hadn't mentioned spending the night, but Leah assumed it would be necessary. A heaviness pressed against her heart as she folded her nightgown and placed it inside the small suitcase. Twice she stopped and took in deep, calming breaths in a desperate effort not to cry. Only God knew how she would manage to stand before a judge and not make an idiot of herself by bursting into tears.

Ten minutes before Cain was due to arrive the doorbell chimed. A sad smile touched Leah's tired expression. Cain was eager to get this over and be done with her. Emotions were warring so fiercely inside her that for one crazy moment she considered throwing herself into his arms, admitting her love and pleading with Cain that they stay married. The insanity passed as quickly as it came.

But it wasn't Cain who was at her door.

"Siggy!" Taken unaware, Leah hadn't time to disguise her surprise. Although he was impeccably dressed in a suit and his ever-present bow tie, Leah could see that he was distressed.

"I didn't mean it, darling. Not a word." He moved past her into the apartment, turned and fiercely hauled her into his arms.

Totally taken by surprise, Leah let out a small cry. "Siggy." Her breath came in a giant gulp. "It's all right. Don't worry about last night." Not knowing exactly what to do with her arms, Leah patted him gently on the back. Siggy buried his face in her neck, his words muffled and incoherent.

A movement behind Leah shocked her into utter stillness.

"I suggest you take your hands off my wife, Harcharik."

Never had Leah heard anything so chilling. Her breath was stopped in her lungs, and she felt the accusing eyes that bored into her shoulder blades.

Immediately Siggy dropped his arms, freeing her, and Leah turned to face the icy rage that contorted Cain's features.

He said nothing, his face as hard as granite and his eyes as cold as ice chips. Speechless, he stood, feet braced, waiting for the slightest opportunity to crush Siggy.

Knowing he had lost, knowing his health was in imminent danger if he proceeded, Siggy cleared his throat and straightened his glasses. "Goodbye, Leah." His voice was low and wavering as he stepped around her, taking short, sliding steps.

"Goodbye, Siggy," she whispered.

Still Cain didn't move. Even after Siggy had left the apartment and closed the door, Cain didn't budge. The controlled fury exuded from him at every pore. His fists clenched and unclenched at his sides as if he remained eager for a fight.

She stepped into her bedroom and returned with the suitcase. Slipping her arms into a light jacket, she met him at the front door. "I'm...I'm ready now," she whispered, her eyes downcast.

"I'll just bet you are," he said with a snarl.

When Leah locked the front door, Cain took the overnight case from her hand and headed to his car, leaving her to follow. It was as if he couldn't get away from her fast enough.

They drove for an hour, and Leah was tempted to demand just where they were headed. The airport, any airport, was miles in the opposite direction. But she was too angry to speak up. When Cain pulled into a huge parking lot, Leah understood. They were at a lake, the name of which she missed. Several float-planes were moored along the dock. Neither of them uttered a word as Cain helped her out of the car and carried her suitcase. Perilously close to tears, Leah followed him down the long, narrow dock to the plane moored at the end.

Two men were waiting for them, and Cain paused to talk for a few minutes. Leah stood back, not wanting to be forced into light conversation with people she didn't know and would never see again. Like Cain, all she wanted was to get this divorce over with, she decided miserably.

Cain returned and helped her into the passenger side of the two-seat Cessna. It became immediately obvious that he was to be their pilot. Leah didn't know he could fly; but then, she doubted that she really knew this man at all.

Like a robot programmed for servitude, she did everything he instructed. Even when he handed her a cup of light coffee, she drank it, although Cain knew that she always had her coffee black. Why argue? What good would it do now?

Leah kept her face averted as they sped over the glassy surface of the lake.

"Don't . . . don't you have to contact an air traffic controller?"

"No," he answered crisply, not glancing her way. "Visual flight rules apply here." His words were clear and precise. The way their relationship should have been. Where did they go wrong? Leah wondered wretchedly. In her mind's eye, she tried to pinpoint the exact minute that they had made their first mistake. An unbearably sad smile touched her eyes. The turning point for them had been the last time they stood before a judge. Now it was just as much of a mistake, and she was helpless to prevent it.

Without a glance in her direction, Cain accelerated the little plane. Leah emitted a soundless gasp as they left the glass-surfaced lake and were cast into the blue heavens. Her tense fingers bit into one another, then gradually relaxed.

Her gaze fell to her clasped hands in her lap. The ring felt heavy and awkward again. Briefly, desperately, she toyed with the idea of telling him that because of her pregnancy her fingers had swollen and she couldn't take the ring off. The thought produced a silent sob that heaved her shoulders.

"You sick?"

"No." She continued looking out the side window, oblivious to the beautiful scenery of the world below. All that stretched before her was boundless blue sky, empty of anything but a few scattered clouds. Leah felt that her life was as empty as the sky, while not nearly as beautiful.

Unconsciously her fingers continued to toy with the wedding band, moving it up and over her knuckle, then sliding it into its rightful position over her long, tapered finger.

"Don't be so damn anxious to take that ring off," he snapped.

Leah froze and dragged her eyes from her hands to stare out the window again. She was utterly desolate and so very tired. The hum of the engine lulled her into a light sleep. With her head propped against the side of the plane, she felt reality slip away as she surrendered to the welcome oblivion. Even in her hazy dreams, though, tears burned the back of her eyes. One must have slipped past the shield of her thick lashes, because Cain gently brushed his finger over the elegant curve of her cheek, waking her. Leah's throat constricted painfully at the tenderness she felt. How unbearably sad it was that she had to be half-asleep for him to demonstrate his gentle nature.

Later, much later, Leah again felt Cain's touch. Only this time it was his whole hand as he ever so carefully laid it over her stomach. A brief smile touched her mouth. She never knew how Cain felt about the baby. When he'd come to her with the pictures, after first discovering her condition, he'd been shocked and concerned. But he'd never said what his feelings were. Would Cain want a hand in their child's upbringing? Holding on to the beautiful thought of Cain with their child in his arms, Leah stirred and sat upright. Her neck ached, and she rubbed some of the soreness away, rotating her head as she massaged the tired muscles. Confident that their baby would have his love—even if she didn't—Leah spoke for the first time.

"How much farther?"

"We're almost there now."

A scan of the area revealed only dense forest below.

"Where's Reno?" Certainly she should be able to see it by now.

"A ways," he answered noncommittally.

"But shouldn't we be within sight of it?"

"No."

Cain began his descent, and Leah searched around her, looking for a place for them to land. As Cain made his sweeping approach, a large lake came into view.

Concerned now, Leah swiveled her gaze to him. "Where are we?"

"A lake."

"I can see that. What are we doing here?"

"Nothing." The plane glided effortlessly onto the smooth surface of the deep blue water. Cain's concentration was centered on controlling their landing.

"We...we aren't going to Reno, are we?" she whispered.

Cain turned and stared at her with eyes that looked into her soul.

"No."

Chapter Eleven

The Cessna coasted to a stop at the large private dock that extended from the shore. A log cabin stood back from the land, its wide porch facing the lake, a rock-hewn chimney jutting out from the shake roof. Overhead, a hawk, its wings spread wide, made a lazy circle above them. Its cry could be heard for miles. Leah sighed at the beauty of the scene. But then she remembered and she stiffened. They were supposed to be in Reno.

"I demand to know where we are." A chill raced up her spine, reminding her she was no longer in the warm desert air of San Diego, but in the mountains.

Cain didn't answer her. Instead he swung open the door of the cockpit and leaped down onto the wooden dock that rocked with the force of his weight. "Are you coming or not?'' Hands on his hips, Cain regarded her idly, giving the impression that it didn't matter to him if she sat in the plane all day.

''Tell me where we are first.''

He hesitated as if debating within himself. ''My home.''

The curiosity to know what awaited her prompted Leah to move. Cain gave her his hand and helped her onto the dock so that she was by his side once again.

''Why are we here? Did you need to pick up something?''

His mouth remained tightly closed as he ignored both Leah and her question. He turned aside, leaving her to follow if she chose.

Leah did. Her gaze fell on the house. This was no simple log cabin, but one of polished pine built by a master craftsman. The wide porch and open door of the two-story structure beckoned her inside.

Timidly, Leah climbed the steps to the porch and came into a huge central room. Sunlight spilled into the room from the open door, setting the interior to glowing.

Cain was kneeling in front of a huge fireplace, whittling off slivers of wood, preparing to start a fire. Briefly, Leah wondered what was wrong with igniting paper, but she didn't ask.

Her thin cotton jacket was no longer sufficient to warm her, and she rubbed her hands over her arms and closed the door. The central room led off to a quaint kitchen with all the modern conveniences.

"You might look around for something to eat," he said without turning around, intent on his task. The sound of a match being struck was followed by the first faint flickerings of the fire.

Leah's gaze wandered to the stairs at the end of the room. Four steps led to a landing and then angled to the left. Cain's photographs covered the cabin walls— if she could call this spacious home a cabin. The landing held his awards. Leah walked up the first series of stairs, and with hands in her pockets to keep her fingers warm, she paused to read the framed certificates. Her heart swelled with pride as she scanned them.

"I thought you were fixing us some lunch." Cain stood and crossed his arms over his broad chest, regarding her curiously.

"I . . . will." Her fingertips ran over one oak frame. "You never told me you won a Pulitzer."

He shrugged carelessly. "I wasn't aware it would impress you."

A lazy smile crinkled the lines about her eyes. "In other words, you'd rather eat than overwhelm me with your credits."

His returning grin was his first smile of the day. "Exactly."

The fire added a cozy warmth to the cabin in quick order. Shortly Leah served them hot tomato soup and turkey sandwiches. They both ate ravenously.

Dabbing the corner of her mouth with the paper napkin, Leah pushed her empty bowl aside. "Are you going to tell me why we're here?"

He regarded her coolly. "I could."

"Then please do. Good heavens, I don't even know where we are."

"That's the way I wanted it."

Leah forced out a light laugh. "You make it sound like you've kidnapped me."

"I have." He inclined his head toward the front door and the plane just outside. "No one knows you're here. Certainly not your precious Sidney, and I have every intention of keeping it that way."

"And just how long do you plan to hold me here?" she inquired stiffly.

"Until the baby comes."

Leah choked out a gasp. "Why, that's months...that's crazy." She couldn't believe what she was hearing. Had the pressures of the Kahu expedition caused Cain to lose his sanity?

"The desperate plan of a desperate man," Cain said in a clipped manner, and stood to pour himself a cup of coffee. He handed her a glass of milk. Twisting the chair around, he straddled it and regarded her as though they'd been discussing football scores.

"You're serious, aren't you?" His declaration was just beginning to sink into her bemused brain.

"Dead serious."

"But why?"

"I told you I didn't want Sidney around my child."

Leah gritted her teeth. "His name is Siggy. Why...why do you insist on calling him that?" Tears blurred her vision. Cain was so full of insane pride and jealous anger that he couldn't see what was right in front of his own two eyes.

Standing, Leah delivered their dirty dishes to the sink. Her arms cradled her stomach as she walked back to the table. "What if I promised not to see Siggy again? Would that convince you to let me go?"

"No."

"Why not?" she cried.

"Because if you have your freedom, you might run away from me. I couldn't take that, Leah. Not with my baby growing inside you." He hand caught her by the waist, bringing her close to his chair so that she had to drop her eyes to meet his gaze. "You once told me my problem was that I didn't care about anything."

A chill that had nothing to do with the room temperature raced up her spine. She recalled the conversation well. They had been planting the sonar equipment when their rubber raft was lifted from the ocean by a playful whale, threatening their lives.

"You were wrong," Cain continued. "I care. I care very deeply for our baby and for you." His hand slipped inside her sweater. He lifted it up at the waist and very gently kissed her smooth, ivory stomach.

Leah's fingers slid through his hair, holding him to her. Tears rolled unheeded down her pale face. "Are you saying—" she whispered with a harsh breath "—that you love me?"

"Dear Lord, I care about you more than anything in my life," Cain breathed.

"Then why... why did you give me back the necklace?" Tears streaked her face and fell onto his shoulders.

Stunned, Cain lifted his head. A myriad of emotions passed over his face as he slowly stood. Taking a clean handkerchief from the back pocket of his jeans, he tenderly wiped the tears from her face.

"Why did you give me back the necklace?" she repeated, almost angry. How could he stand there with his eyes full of love when he'd practically shoved her into Siggy's arms?

"Why did you take it? I was asking you to make your choice between Harcharik and me."

"Choice?" Leah echoed in disbelief. "I...I thought you were telling me that...that what we shared was over. That the time had come to go back to our lives and that Siggy was part of my life...and you weren't."

"Are you crazy?" His eyes narrowed with a dark frown.

"Yes," she shouted, breaking free of his embrace. "Crazy enough to have married you and even crazier to have fallen in love with you."

Cain stiffened and raked a hand through his hair. "You love me?" he asked in a low, wondrous voice as if he couldn't believe what she'd said.

"Oh, Cain," she sobbed. "How could you have known me so intimately and not know me at all?"

He looked so stunned, so utterly taken aback, that Leah had to laugh.

"Could I have given myself to you so freely without involving my heart?" Leah asked softly.

"But . . ." he stammered.

"Do you love me?" He'd said he cared, but caring and loving were two different things.

Cain's features hardened until they were sharp and intense. "Are you crazy?"

Leah smiled. "I believe I already answered that question."

Reaching for her, Cain held her so close she could barely breathe. "I love you, Leah Talmadge Hawkins. I think I'd rather live the life of a hermit than be without you."

"How could we have been so stupid?" she asked, winding her arms around his neck. "Oh, Cain, hold me. Promise me that you'll never let me go. Not for any reason."

Swinging her into his arms, he looked adoringly into her eyes. "Are you crazy?"

Laughing, crying, Leah looped her arms around his neck and spread kisses over his face. Her lips found his jaw, his temple, his eyes and nose, lingering every place but his lips.

A low growl escaped from his throat as he paused on the landing. "I'm hoping that by the time we reach the bedroom your aim will improve, Mrs. Hawkins."

"I may require more practice," she teased, bringing her mouth a scant inch from his.

"A lifetime, my love, a lifetime."

Sometime later, Leah propped her head on her hand and basked in the lambent glow of love coming from her husband's eyes.

"I love you," he whispered, kissing the tips of her fingers. "I plan to spend the rest of my life proving it to you again and again."

"You just did." Ever so gently she pressed a kiss to his lips.

"Would you be angry if I got out my camera and took your picture? Dear Lord, I've never seen a woman more beautiful than you are at this moment."

A soft, radiant smile lit up her hazel eyes. "I think I could get to be very jealous of that camera of yours."

Surprise flickered from the depths of his dark eyes. "You needn't worry, love. Ever. Nothing will stand between us again, and certainly not my camera."

Not for a moment did Leah doubt him. At one time in his life, Cain had needed the camera because pictures revealed the emotions that he couldn't. Love had changed that.

Twisting around so that he was braced above her, he gently brushed the hair from her face. "We've never talked about the baby," he said on a sober note. "Are you unhappy?"

Her eyes widened with incandescent wonder. "I don't think I've ever been more delighted about anything in my life. I wanted to shout it from the highest mountain." She wound her arms around his neck and planted a lingering kiss on his parted lips. Averting her eyes, she tenderly brushed the hair from his temple.

"What about you? How did you feel about...the baby?"

He chuckled. "You mean after I got over being furious that you hadn't told me?"

She nodded, still not meeting his gaze.

He paused and grew so still that Leah's heart lurched. "You want the truth, I suppose."

"Yes," she whispered.

"I got down on my knees and thanked God. I've never been more grateful for anything. I knew that if you were pregnant, then you might be willing to give our marriage a second chance. And if worse came to worst and you didn't, then I would still have a tangible part of you through our child."

"Oh, Cain, I do love you so." Now, finally, with his arms wrapped securely around her, Leah could believe that this wonderful, loving man was hers. Completely, totally, utterly hers.

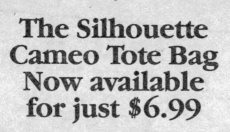

The Silhouette Cameo Tote Bag Now available for just $6.99

Handsomely designed in blue and bright pink, its stylish good looks make the Cameo Tote Bag an attractive accessory. The Cameo Tote Bag is big and roomy (13″ square), with reinforced handles and a snap-shut top. You can buy the Cameo Tote Bag for $6.99, plus $1.50 for postage and handling.

Send your name and address with check or money order for $6.99 (plus $1.50 postage and handling), a total of $8.49 to:

**Silhouette Books
120 Brighton Road
P.O. Box 5084
Clifton, NJ 07015-5084
ATTN: Tote Bag**

SIL-T-1

The Silhouette Cameo Tote Bag can be purchased pre-paid only. No charges will be accepted. Please allow 4 to 6 weeks for delivery.

Arizona and N.Y. State Residents Please Add Sales Tax

Offer not available in Canada.

Take 4
Silhouette Special Edition novels
FREE...

and preview future books in your home for 15 days!

Start with 4 FREE books, yours to keep. Then, preview 6 brand-new Special Edition® novels—delivered right to your door every month—as soon as they are published.

When you decide to keep them, pay just $1.95 each ($2.50 each in Canada), *with no shipping, handling, or other additional charges of any kind!*

Romance *is* alive, well and flourishing in the moving love stories presented by Silhouette Special Edition. They'll awaken your desires, enliven your senses, and leave you tingling all over with excitement. In each romance-filled story you'll live and breathe the emotions of love and the satisfaction of romance triumphant.

You won't want to miss a single one of the heart-felt stories presented by Silhouette Special Edition; and when you take advantage of this special offer, you won't have to.

You'll also receive a FREE subscription to the Silhouette Books Newsletter as long as you remain a member. Each lively issue is filled with news on upcoming titles, interviews with your favorite authors, even their favorite recipes.

To become a home subscriber and receive your first 4 books FREE, fill out and mail the coupon today!

Silhouette Special Edition®

Silhouette Books, 120 Brighton Rd., P.O. Box 5084, Clifton, NJ 07015-5084

AM-TRIB-1

AMERICAN TRIBUTE

RIGHT BEHIND THE RAIN
Elaine Camp #301—April 1986
The difficulty of coping with her brother's
death brought reporter Raleigh Torrence
to the office of Evan Younger, a police
psychologist. He helped her to deal with
her feelings and emotions, including love.

CHEROKEE FIRE
Gena Dalton #307—May 1986
It was Sabrina Dante's silver spoon that
Cherokee cowboy Jarod Redfeather couldn't
trust. The two lovers came from opposite
worlds, but Jarod's Indian heritage taught
them to overcome their differences.

NOBODY'S FOOL
Renee Roszel #313—June 1986
Everyone bet that Martin Dante and Cara
Torrence would get together. But Martin
wasn't putting any money down, and Cara
was out to prove that she was nobody's fool.

MISTY MORNINGS, MAGIC NIGHTS
Ada Steward #319—July 1986
The last thing Carole Stockton wanted was to
fall in love with another politician, especially
Donnelly Wakefield. But under a blanket of
secrecy, far from the campaign spotlights,
their love became a powerful force.

COMING NEXT MONTH

THE INFAMOUS MADAM X—Joan Smith
Winning the auto show became a slim possibility when Brett plowed into "Madam X"—Mila's antique Cadillac. She was angry at first, but like the roar of a powerful engine, the heat of passion eventually exploded.

LOOKALIKE LOVE—Nancy John
Cleo agreed to model for a new advertising campaign because she was an exact lookalike of the original model. She didn't know charading as Kent's girlfriend was part of the contract.

IRISH EYES—Lynnette Morland
Roberta was on the brink of superstardom, until Irish chauvinist Christy O'Laighleis arrived. He claimed she was the American enemy sent to export Irish talent—and he would do anything to stop her!

DARLING DETECTIVE—Karen Young
Sidney was an ace financial detective. But Beau didn't think women and business mixed. While unmuddling his finances, maybe she could also teach him a thing or two about the business of love.

TALL, DARK AND HANDSOME—Glenda Sands
They were too different—the playboy and the prude. Juliet's values and life-style could never blend with Morgan Jay Stanton's. But it's not always easy to resist such sweet temptation.

STOLEN PROMISE—Christine Flynn
Was Britt really innocent of involvement with the art thefts? Creed wanted to believe her, despite the evidence against her. He didn't put her behind bars, but her heart was being held captive.

AVAILABLE THIS MONTH:

TO CATCH A THIEF
Brittany Young

WILD HORIZONS
Frances Lloyd

YESTERDAY'S HERO
Debbie Macomber

ROSES NEVER FADE
Raye Morgan

A MAN OF CHARACTER
Barbara Bartholomew

ANGEL AND THE SAINT
Emilie Richards